MW00682140

WRITERS REPUBLIC

Avalon's Vault

M. E. CASTANARES

WRITERS REPUBLIC L.L.C.
515 Summit Ave. Unit R1
Union City, NJ 07087, USA

Website: *www.writersrepublic.com*
Hotline: *1-877-656-6838*
Email: *info@writersrepublic.com*

Ordering Information:
Quantity sales. Special discounts are available on quantity purchases by corporations, associations, and others. For details, contact the publisher at the address above.

Library of Congress Control Number: 2021930165
ISBN-13:   978-1-63728-120-8   [Paperback Edition]
                  978-1-63728-121-5   [Digital Edition]

Rev. date: 01/04/2021

This book is dedicated to my mother
ROMANA (NAYRE) CASTANARES

Prologue

*E*veryone watched as Emily's body began to glow just as Daniel's did. Serena continued to read from the book, and as she did, the light grew brighter and brighter until Emily's body was completely engulfed in a white luminescent brilliance.

Serena's words grew louder and louder. Suddenly, a flash of light came from Emily's body that caused everyone to shield their eyes. When the flash subsided, the onlookers rubbed their eyes, hoping to regain their focus. And like a ghostly apparition amidst a white backdrop, Emily walked toward them.

Chapter

1

It's 2:00 a.m., and I had the dream again, creating yet another restless night. I saw the same images and the same strange place I had been seeing each night I fell asleep. The dream would begin with flashes of different colors. A blurry blend of red, yellow, blue, green, and purple cycled into one another as if looking through a kaleidoscope. And as the colors faded, I saw what I first thought to be a castle that stood high upon a mountain surrounded by a forest of green, looking majestic amongst the white floating clouds. Below, a calming river flowed up to the greenery's rocky edge. The more I saw this place, the more I became overwhelmed with the feeling of strength and power. It was then I realized this place I have never seen before was a fortress. I awoke abruptly and sat up on my bed, staring at the darkness of my room. Tonight's dream had a different feeling and, this time, appeared more vivid.

I wish I knew what it all meant, I thought.

I was too awake to fall back to sleep, so I reached beneath my bed to find what used to be my treasure chest of memories. It was my memory book. As I flipped through the pages to the photos taken after the caverns, I saw the book in its entirety. I was looking at a completed puzzle. The lost years without my mother were regained, and the long-lost smile that had faded from my father's face was back. It had been a little over three years since Serena brought me back from the dead. My father is now human, no longer immortal, and I have my mother back. I am now an adult, slightly two months past my eighteenth birthday. My family's new life continued in our Atlantic City, New Jersey, home; and it is there we had spent these years and months, making up for all our lost time. I have enjoyed every moment with my mother, as we discussed our missing years and what our plans were for the future. It is a future I never thought I could imagine, but here it is, like bricks to a pavement, ready to be laid and put into place. I saw my parents starting to lay their bricks, their foundation for a future, I now began to wonder what path my life was to take. As I closed the book belonging to my photo memories, I had cherished over the years, I felt as though I was closing a chapter to one part of my life. I pondered whether this forthcoming new chapter was to have new options like college or some type of profession that I should be looking forward to. However, something intrinsic was telling me otherwise. I could feel myself changing, and I wished it was just the move from adolescence into a young adulthood; it was something more. There was something inside me just waiting to emerge. If my dreams were to be the gateway to my true path, then my only fear was the unknown. My name is Emily Castle, and here is my story about how and why I became an immortal.

"Daniel, can you bring all those bags into the kitchen for me?" asked Ellie while holding her belly.

"Ellie, the baby shower is only supposed to be a few guests," Daniel said, as he swung bag after bag over his shoulder and lugged them through the hallway.

"Yes, I know but I may have tweaked the guest list just a bit after hearing from a few old friends," said Ellie with a giggle.

"Okay, so tell me again why we let Ms. Pike go on vacation during all this party planning? You know, with you eight and half months along, Cy constantly working in his lab, and Emily who knows where these days, a lot of the grunt work will fall on me," Daniel stated as he plopped the bags onto the kitchen floor.

"Oh, stop complaining," laughed Ellie.

"How sure are you about this? Because last time I checked, your party planning skills were sort of subpar." Daniel gently conveyed to Ellie, "I mean the last time you decided to plan anything…it didn't quite end very well."

"I have to agree with Daniel on this," Cy added, walking into the kitchen.

"Seriously, I'm feeling a bit ganged up here. Have you no confidence in my skills?" said Ellie, waving her hands in the air.

Cy grabbed two beers from the fridge, cracked open both bottles, and handed one to Daniel. Both men took a drink together, put their bottles down on the counter at the same time, and in unison replied, "No, not really," with a smirk.

"Ellie, honey, you have other amazing skills. But party planning is just not high on your aptitude list," Daniel said, as he moved behind Ellie and wrapped his arms around her protruding waist.

"We need to call Ms. Pike and have her come home. She has already been gone for weeks," said Daniel.

"I second that motion," added Cy as he finished off his beer.

"Motion carried," sighed Ellie in defeat. "I know you gents are right, and I love you for your honesty. Call Ms. Pike so she can come home and work on the party planning. I will only work on the guest list. By the way, has anyone seen Em lately? I just thought she would be interested in helping. It's not like her to be absent a lot lately," questioned Ellie.

"Maybe she is in her darkroom?" added Daniel.

"Actually, I just passed it on my way to the kitchen, hoping to find her there too, but no Emily. When I heard voices in the kitchen, I thought she was here with you," Cy recalled, "By the way, how is Emily adjusting to all these new changes, especially about having a new baby sister very soon?" added Cy.

"We talked about it at the beginning of our pregnancy, both Daniel and I wanted to make sure she was going to be okay with our new future," Ellie said.

"Yes, and she was overjoyed by the entire idea. She was happy with me being human now. And she agreed the greatest gift ever granted to me was the chance to be a father," explained Daniel.

"Maybe she is bored?" laughed Cy, finishing the last swig of his drink.

"What do you mean?" Ellie asked.

"Well, you have to admit, Emily has lived a unique life whilst growing up. She has been on many adventures with both of you and has been raised unlike any normal teenager has. Now your lives will calm down and be more settled for the sake of your new one coming. Maybe she is not ready to settle down and live the content life you both have chosen. Her path is still yet to be determined," said Cy.

"Okay I can see your point, Cy. But between the three of us, have you noticed anything different about Em lately? I mean, ever since the caverns?" Ellie questioned.

"What are you saying?" Daniel asked.

"I know my daughter, and the moment I thought we lost her forever in the caverns was the worst moment in my life. And the moment she was back and alive, I knew it was her. Even though she was brought back to life by magic, it was still her. But these past few months, something has been off. She has been different. I don't know how to explain it," said Ellie.

"Well, I have noticed she has stopped taking photos and working in her darkroom," added Cy. "There has been no smell of her chemicals as of late."

"I have heard her up late at night. Sometimes in her room or moving around downstairs. And aside from being very quiet and pensive lately, she seems like herself to me. Maybe she is just growing up and we just need to give her some space to figure out her future. You know, like what Cy was explaining," Daniel said.

"Maybe I am overthinking this. Or call it a mother's instinct. I think some one-on-one time with my daughter is needed. I'll call her," stated Ellie, as she reached for her cell phone in her purse.

Ellie proceeded to dial Emily's cell number. Ellie could hear the ring from Emily's end, but the connection only went to voice mail. Ellie repeated the process, hoping a second attempt would get a connection; however, once again, no answer, just Emily's voice mail.

"She is not answering. Why can't I reach her?" wondered Ellie, slowly growing concerned.

Chapter

2

The ocean was calm with gentle waves breaking against the rocks. It was midday. I spent a great deal of time here at the cove just thinking and hoping for answers. The cove was my new sanctuary, and it seemed to replace my darkroom lately. Every time I visited the cove, I hoped to be alone with my thoughts, but strange voices that I assumed came from my head were distracting me. Oddly enough, I was not afraid of it. Like my nightly dreams, the voices are proving to act like my internal compass, leading me to my north star.

I stumbled upon this place one day while I was taking scenic photos for a school project. I was instantly attracted to its secrecy. To find it, you had to travel down a hidden narrow gravel path that led to a series of rocks by the shore; and once you climbed over the rocks, your feet came to the edge of a small patch of beach and its brown gritty sand. This was my cove. About ten meters across the cove stood a barrier of larger rocks, where most of the waves found their breaking points. And what connected my side to the other was a small cave that would disappear during high tide and reappear during the low tide. The current between both sides was strong, especially closer to the larger rocks, so I knew to avoid those areas. The water was slightly over eight feet deep; basically, it was shallow enough for the currents to run with force and deep enough to pull you under. My mother always said I was a strong swimmer; I suppose she was right. Being by the water, for me, over these past months was my new haven because here, I felt connected to its sound and movements. The open space and the overwhelming draw to nature was inexplicable. I just knew I needed to be here, or maybe someone was telling me to be here. It was almost as if there was another voice speaking to me. Most of the time, I am at my cove. I am alone and rarely see people around. However, today was different.

While I was sitting at my usual place on the sand, I noticed a shadow across the cove. The shadow was drawing closer to the rocks. I continued to watch as the shadow turned into a figure of a young man in jeans and a bright-red shirt. He had short light-brown hair, tanned skin like he had been in the sun all day, and stood about six feet tall, with a lean muscular build. I watched as he wobbled deliriously toward the rocks edge.

"Hey, watch out!" I yelled.

I assumed he would stop once he got to the edge, but instead, he gave a loud moan; and within seconds, the splash into the water filled my heart with dread.

"Oh no! Hey! You okay!" I yelled, jumping from my sandy perch, heading toward the beach's edge.

From my distance, I saw the man's head surface briefly then dip back down into the water. I could see the current slowly pushing him toward my beach; I had no choice. I dropped my bag onto the sand, threw off my shoes, and dove into the water toward the young man's waving hands that breached the water now and again. When I came to the area, I last saw the flailing hands. I stopped swimming and dove beneath the water to see if he submerged again. While underwater, I struggled to find him. I dove a couple more times beneath and finally caught a glimpse of his red shirt sinking near the bottom. I surfaced only to gulp one last breath of air before heading down to the bottom toward the red shirt.

Finding a good grip on some piece of his clothing, I pulled him toward me and continued to swim to the surface toward the beach. With whatever strength I had, I managed to pull him onto my small beach. I checked his pulse and noticed it was there but faint. I began CPR.

After a few rounds of chest compressions and airway breathing, the stranger coughed and released the water trapped in his throat. I turned him onto his side to clear his lungs, hoping he would stay conscious.

He was lucid but screaming in pain. When I turned him on his back, I noticed he had gashes on this head, most likely from the fall at the rocks, along with deep scrapes on his arms. However, it was when I lifted his shirt that I noticed another wound that seemed unrelated to his fall. Even though the wounds were severe, it was the one beneath his shirt that urged me to find my phone and quickly dial the number that last called me.

Within seconds, my mother's voice answered on the other line.

—⟋⟍—

"Emily where have you been? I just tried calling you," shouted Ellie.

"Mom, you can yell at me later, but right now, I need Cy to track my phone. I need help! Someone is badly hurt," Emily cried as she left her phone and went back to the fellow.

Ellie called out to Cy, who already made his way to his laptop and began the trace on Emily's phone.

"I got her. She's at No Man's Cove," Cy urged as he and Daniel dashed for the door.

—⟋⟍—

Still hovering over the stranger's body, I continued to apply pressure on areas where the bleeding wouldn't stop with pieces of clothing I ripped from my jacket and pants. His wounds were too deep; the blood kept pouring out and seeping through the medical bandages I had made. I couldn't stop it, and he was still in agony. I started to panic because I wasn't sure how long it would take for Cy to find me. And I feared this stranger, whose name I didn't even know, was going to die. I pleaded for him to hold on and reassured him that he would be okay. But how would he be okay without medical attention?

Just then, I heard something so strange it should have frightened me; however, it didn't, *"Close your eyes,"* whispered a voice that sounded like the winds were speaking. *"Lay your hands on his wounds,"* whistled the voice again.

I was unsure where the voice was coming from, but I felt it was close by, almost as if it came from within me. I closed my eyes, and with a calming breath, I laid my hands on his wounds. I placed one hand on his chest and the other on his head. Suddenly, I felt light-headed, and all I could hear was the sound of the wind and waves breaking against the rocks merging into one voice. The voice spoke words that I have never heard before. Then a surge of energy began to build from my head to my hands. I opened my eyes and saw that my hands were glowing in a bright-yellow hue. I could feel the wave of energy flowing through me as the light from my hands grew brighter and brighter. The light lasted only a little over a minute, and as the wave of energy slowly subsided, so did the light. I lifted my hands to find the stranger's wounds no longer soaking in blood, no longer open and deep. The wounds were healed, leaving behind only scars. The stranger stabilized and grew calmer. It was as if his pain was taken away.

"Thank you," mumbled the stranger.

"Rest now," I said, still in awe about what I had just did. "What is your name?" I asked, trying to keep him awake for transport.

"My name is Sam," the young man whispered.

I looked down at my hands; they looked the same as they did before the glow, and then I looked at Sam. I had no words to explain what I had just seen. I was completely confused. In the distance, I could clearly hear Cy and my father shouting my name. I called back out to them, "I'm down here."

The ride from the beach to the mansion was quieter than I had expected. Once my father discovered it was not me that was wounded and that I was one the doing the rescuing, he sat proudly in the front, driving the medical van home. In the back, I sat with Cy. The van was installed with all the basic EMS equipment any medical vehicle would require; even the gurney Sam lay on was medical standard. Cy hooked Sam up to the portable blood pressure monitor to check his vitals. Cy also noticed Sam was dehydrated, so he set up a small bag of saline solution near Sam and began infusing it through his arm.

"Looks like your friend here is going to be fine. I gave him some pain meds, that should put him out for a few hours till we get home," concluded Cy, checking readings on the machines, "Now, let's look at you, Emily," continued Cy.

"I'm okay. I swear. This is all Sam's blood," I said, holding up my shirt.

"So, if this is Sam's blood, then why am I not breaking out the bandages and gauzes? I see no open wounds on this fellow, and you are wearing quite a lot of blood. Care to explain?" added Cy.

"Cy, I wish I could. I mean, all I can do is tell you what happened," I said, shrugging my shoulders.

"Okay, please proceed. I would really like to hear this," said Cy, crossing his arms.

"Well, after I saved Sam from the water, I pulled him onto the beach and had to perform CPR. When I was able to revive him, he was in so much pain. Most of the pain I noticed were from wounds caused by the fall onto the rocks. He had these huge gashes on his head and arms, the bleeding was constant," I said as Cy examined Sam's head and arms and noticed the scars.

"So, where did he get these?" asked Cy, referring to the scars.

"They were his wounds," I said apprehensively, "that turned into the scars."

"Emily, wounds don't quickly heal, even with medical attention. We just found you about twenty minutes ago," Cy added.

I paused before I decided to tell Cy the entire truth, or the reality of the truth I knew it to be.

"I think I healed him," I confessed.

"You what? How?" questioned Cy.

"All I know is I laid my hands on his wounds. And when I did, my hands started to glow. Next thing I know, Sam's wounds were all healed, leaving only a scar," I said, deciding not to tell him about the voice I also heard.

"Your hands started to glow? Really?" questioned Cy with a look of suspicion.

"Yes, and I could feel some kind of energy flow through me while my hands were glowing," I said. "It was the most strangest feeling I have ever experienced. And I still don't know how I did it. I really don't know Cy," I pleaded.

"Has this ever happened to you before?" asked Cy

"No! Never!" I said. "I am not sure if I could do it again."

"Hmmm. I guess we will continue this conversation when we get home. Your parents will need to hear this," Cy concluded, with a perplexed expression.

"Oh wait! There was one more thing I wanted to show you that was also odd," I said, sliding over to Sam to lift his shirt, exposing his abdomen. "Take a look at this," I said, motioning Cy to examine.

"That scar looks like..." Cy paused and then reexamined the area adjusting his glasses "A bite mark," Cy added.

"Yes, and it was fresh when I pulled him out of the water. Cy, I could see the teeth impressions in his skin. Whatever animal did this to him was big. That's when I called for help. What do you think did this?" I asked Cy.

"I am not sure. But the scar shows teeth marks made by an animal. I could run some tests when we get him home," said Cy.

"I was hoping you would say that," I added.

"How are things going back there?" yelled my father from a small sliding door leading to the driver's seat.

"All good," replied Cy.

"We are nearly home, so you might want to prepare him for transport. Emily, you good?" asked my father.

"Yes, I'm fine, Father. Cy and I have some something very interesting to share with you, trust me," I replied.

"Emily is not joking Daniel, we have somehow stumbled into something intriguing," said Cy.

"Really?" said my father, very curious.

Chapter

3

The mansion stood tall upon a small hill, with a long driveway that led into a circle. In the center of the circle stood a stone-carved water fountain with a statue of a mermaid holding a giant shell. The opening of the shell gave way to flowing water. It was almost as if the mermaid was pouring water out of the shell and into the base of the fountain. It was nearing dusk, and the surrounding white fountain lights turned on while the green and red fountain lights within the walls of the base of the statue began their illuminating cycle as well. The mermaid statue glowed in a green-reddish hue, which were all created by its strategic lighting effects. I always admired this dreamy, picturesque view of the mansion upon approach every sunset.

The van drove up the long, winding, curved driveway and pulled up to the front doorsteps. Sam was still groggy from the sedative Cy gave him, so we kept him on the gurney and wheeled him into the house and down to Cy's lab. One by one, Cy, Daniel, and myself walked through the doorway. When my mother saw me covered in bloodstains, she instantly reacted.

"Emily, are you hurt?" asked my mother.

"No, Mom, this is not my blood, this is Sam's," I said.

"Is he hurt?" asked my mother.

"Well, not anymore. Let me just go upstairs, clean up, and I will explain later. I promise," I said, easing my mother's growing concerns.

"Don't worry, Ellie, I thought the same thing when I first saw her too. But she wasn't the one in trouble. She was the one who did the rescuing," added Daniel, holding Ellie's shoulders.

"You look somehow proud considering our daughter is covered in blood and ripped clothing," said Ellie as she looked up at Daniel.

"She's following in our footsteps. It's hard not to be." Daniel smiled.

"Yes, but our footsteps sometimes tend to lead us down dangerous paths, remember?" added Ellie. "It's hard for me to think Emily wants that."

"Ellie, after all that we have been through, it's time for you to trust her. I do," Daniel stated.

"Daniel!" boomed Cy's voice from the intercom. "You have to come and see this."

Daniel gave Ellie a soft kiss on the cheek before leaving her side and quickly headed toward Cy's lab. Ellie stood in the foyer, trying to digest what Daniel had said. *How do I let her grow up?* Ellie thought as she motioned to close the door that was left open; she felt the door push back. Someone was entering the house, someone who always seemed to know when she would be needed. As Ellie pulled the door open, her face lit up with surprise to find Ms. Pike walking through the doorway, carrying her two weeks of luggage.

"Hello, dear." Ms. Pike smiled.

"Ms. Pike, what are you doing home?" asked Ellie, surprised.

"Well, I felt like I was gone long enough. And usually, with this household, nothing stays normal for very long," said Ms. Pike.

"Hahaha. Oh, you have such great timing!" Ellie smiled, leaning in to give Ms. Pike a hug. "We were actually going to call you to come home."

"So, how are you feeling these days, dear?" asked Ms. Pike as she loaded the last of her belongings into the living room.

"I'm fine. The baby is fine. But it looks like everyone else has some goings-on, happening today at least," added Ellie, making her way to the couch to rest her legs.

"I knew I smelt something stirring when I walked in the door," said Ms. Pike. "Where is everyone?"

"Daniel and Cy are in the lab with a new friend of Emily's, who apparently was injured or got injured and Emily rescued. I'm still waiting for more details on that. And as for Emily, she is upstairs, cleaning up. She was covered in bloodstains," recalled Ellie.

"Oh my…is Emily all right?" asked Ms. Pike.

"Emily is fine. The blood was from her friend and not her. That part I do know," said Ellie.

"Whew! Thank the stars," exclaimed Ms. Pike. "Let me finish putting away my stuff, get settled back in, and then I can make us all some tea."

"Oh, tea would be wonderful. Thank you. Yes, you go right ahead and finish up. I will work on moving this whale-like body of mine to Cy's lab and see what is going on there. Oh, by the way, while you are upstairs, can you also check on Emily for me?" asked Ellie, struggling to lift herself from the couch.

"Sure thing, dear," replied Ms. Pike as she gently aided Ellie's ascent from the couch and watched her waddle her way toward the lab.

Cy's lab was enormous. It inhabited the entire lower level of the house and had its own elevator. Half of the room had walls that were covered in flat LED screens that connected to large computer drives and keyboards. Cy's workbench always had some invention being worked on—currently, it was some replicating device. In the middle of the lab's technological hub stood a large black marble table, known to all as the brain. Everything from the drives to the screens could feed into this table and project in 3D any information needed. The brain table had a built-in touch pad that, if given the right command, would activate and access anything in the lab. The other half of the lab was more of Cy's science/medical section where test tubes, microscopes, and analyzing machines resided. It was a combination of science and technology, with a dash of science fiction that decorated Cy's abode. Ellie gracefully made her way to Cy's lab, and from the elevator hallway, she could overhear the two men discussing. Curious, Ellie moved quickly to try and join their discussion.

"I have analyzed the scar tissue, and I can definitely deduce that it was an animal that attacked him," Cy stated, moving from his work chair computer to the Brain Table. Cy activated the Brain Table and produced an enlarged image of the scar for Daniel to examine.

"I agree. There's no human teeth markings on this bite," Daniel said.

"Based on the shape and density of the bite, I have to say it's most likely canine than anything," Cy added.

"You mean like a dog?" asked Ellie, joining the conversation.

"No, bigger. Much bigger," added Cy.

"What could be bigger than a dog?" questioned Ellie. "And where did you say Emily found this guy again?"

"She came across him at No Man's Cove," said Cy.

"There's a lot of dense forests around there. And people usually like to camp in those woods too. I used to wander through there at night, when I was a vampire. I also helped the park ranger track down campers who lost their way, once or twice. So I know that area. I can connect with my ranger friend and see if they know of any animal attacks lately," said Daniel.

"That's a good idea," agreed Cy. "I can connect to one of my satellite uplinks and see if we can get a topical view of that area. I can set the computer to scan for large animal gatherings," Cy added.

"Or we can just ask him," Ellie interjected, pointing to the young man gaining consciousness.

Both Daniel and Cy joined Ellie's glance at the awakening Sam.

"Where am I?" asked Sam, rubbing his eyes.

"You are in my lab." said Cy as he helped Sam sit upright on the gurney.

"Lab? Why am I in a lab?" Sam questioned as he observed his surroundings for the first time.

"Take it easy. What do you remember last?" asked Ellie.

"I remember falling into water. There was a lot of water around me, and I think I was drowning. Then I blacked out. When I came to, there was a girl. I was in so much pain and there was blood everywhere. The girl put her hands on me, and I could feel a wave of heat run through my entire body. Then there was no more pain," Sam recalled.

"So, are you saying that you were suddenly healed?" asked Cy, recalling Emily's explanation in the medical van.

"I-I must have been," stuttered Sam. "I was bleeding, and then I wasn't," said Sam.

Sam lifted his shirt and reached for the wound that left him in so much pain just a few hours ago. When he noticed the scar instead on his abdomen, he was bewildered. "*What? How?*"

Daniel and Ellie turned toward each other, and without even uttering a single word, they both knew something was happening with their daughter.

Sam glanced back at the friendly strangers around him and asked, "So, who are you all anyway? I mean, names would be a good start."

"I'm sorry, this must be odd for you," said Ellie with a smile, "My name is Ellie Castle-Sangelos, this is Daniel, my husband, and that is Cypres Migill," informed Ellie.

Sam casually nodded in the direction of each person and asked, "Is the girl here too? Who is she? I think I owe her my life."

"The girl you met on the beach is my daughter, Emily," added Ellie. "She is here, just upstairs cleaning up. I'm sure you will meet her later."

"Sounds good. Do you know of any inexpensive hotels I can stay at? I just got into town, and after the attack, well… I was not able to find one," said Sam, reaching for his back pocket. To his surprise, his wallet was still there and intact.

"Attack?" questioned Daniel.

"Yeah, that is how I got this," said Sam, pointing to the bite scar.

"What do you remember about your attack?" asked Cy.

"It happened last night, really late in the evening, still a few hours before dawn. I remember the full moon was out, and I thought how lucky I am because it made the night sky so bright. I always liked camping under a full moon. That day, I had planned to hike the trails in the woods and then camp out for my first night. Back home in North Dakota, I always felt at home being outdoors," said Sam.

"You were camping alone?" interjected Daniel.

"Yes, don't worry, I am used to it. I enjoy being outdoors. My grandfather was part-Sioux and taught me how to fish, hunt, and track in the woods," replied Sam.

"You're pretty young to be traveling alone," said Ellie.

"Well, I kind of have been on my own since my parents died when I was about eight years old. My grandfather was the one who ended up raising me. He taught me how to fend for myself. It was a hard lesson at times, but you learn from your mistakes and grow up pretty fast when it is only yourself to depend on," said Sam.

"Can we please let the boy continue with his story about the attack?" interrupted Cy, "I, for one, am still very curious about the bite mark."

"Right, back to the attack," added Daniel. "Please continue, Sam,"

Sam cleared his throat and continued with his story. "I had finished my hike in the woods and was finding a good place to camp. I came across a small clearing perfect to set up. While I was pitching my tent and settling in for the night, I had this strange feeling someone was watching me. You know, that feeling you get when you know you are alone, but something inside tells you maybe you are not. Anyways, during my hike, I had found this small wooden box wedged between some tree trunks. It looked like it had been there for ages, so I decided to bring it with me. Sitting by the fire, I pulled the wooden box from my bag and carefully examined it. With the extra light from the moon, the blaze of the campfire, and my small handheld flashlight, I had more than enough light to clearly see it. I remember the lock looked so old but solid. I grabbed a rock and used it to break the lock open. I was surprised that I was able to break through with one swing. I opened the box and found what looked to be an indigo-blue-colored, wine-shaped bottle encased inside. Just as I was about to attempt to remove the cork and look inside, I suddenly heard a deep growling noise. Startled, the bottle slipped from my hands and fell to the grass. I quickly turned around and saw nothing. But when I turned back toward the fire, there it was," said Sam.

"What was it?" asked Cy

"At first, I thought it was a bear, but then I saw its teeth and fangs as it moved into the fire's light. It was the biggest wolf I had ever seen," said Sam, holding his hands apart, giving his listeners the impression of size.

"A wolf?" Daniel added.

"Yes," replied Sam.

"What did you do next?" asked Ellie.

"What could I do? I was paralyzed. I couldn't move. I watched in complete fear as the animal drew closer. I looked around for something to defend myself with—a log or branch—but all I had was the wooden box at my feet. The animal continued to growl at me, and I feared it was getting ready to attack. Just then, the wolf lunged at my face. I quickly grabbed the box to block the canine's teeth that were just inches from my head. The wolf's jaw broke into the box, and in its crushing blow, half the box remained lodged in its fangs. While the animal struggled to remove the box from its jaw, I saw it as my chance to run. And I ran. I bolted into the woods, leaving behind all my belongings. I heard the animal howl and then start to chase me. There was some distance between us, but it was not enough. The animal's giant legs closed the gap as I heard its thundering paws hitting the ground behind me. I just kept running. I ran toward the sound I heard earlier in the day. The sound was growing louder, so I knew it was close. I just had to make it down one last hill and there it would be. I was about halfway to the base of the hill when I looked back and noticed my animal attacker perched at the top of the hill. It leaped down and began its charge. I must have accidentally slipped on something because suddenly, I was tumbling down toward the base of the hill. The fall left me winded and badly bruised. The sound of rapids from the river was much closer now. The river was where I needed to be. While lying on my back, I thought if I could only get to the part of the river where I left my boat tied, I would be safe, so I struggled to my feet. But the animal had other plans. I heard its growl again, even louder now as it leaped on top of me. I remember screaming in terror as I saw its jaw open and moved to clench its teeth into my stomach. Somehow, I remember getting my legs underneath its belly, and as it was just about to bite down, I lifted the weight of the animal with my legs and pushed it off me. The animal's furry body flew off me, but not far enough as I could feel its paw pull me toward it. What I didn't know was I was at the wrong end of the river. My boat was on the other end. This end of the river had a drop-off where below, several rivers converged into one massive rapid. The animal and I continued to roll down a small slope heading toward the cliff's edge where the rivers' raging waters churned below. I was entangled in its fur, and the battle to avoid its teeth that were chomping at my side seemed endless.

I needed to get this animal off me, I needed to get free. Moments before reaching the edge of the cliff, I remember grabbing onto a large root from a tree. My quick grab onto the root stopped my descent off the cliff as the sound of water crashed below. The animal was not so lucky. I watched as it rolled off the cliff and into the white crashing waters. I heard it howl and then a splash. It was then I felt the sharp pain at my side. It had bitten me just before it went over," concluded Sam.

"Wow!" exclaimed Ellie. "I am so sorry you had to go through that."

"But you were miles away from Emily's cove, how did you end up near her little beach?" asked Cy.

"That part is somewhat blurry, but I do remember walking along the river until I came to the end where my boat was. I think I paddled downstream for a bit and then passed out from exhaustion. While I was out, the boat just drifted with the current. I remember waking up to daylight and the sun on my face. I really don't know how I got to the cove. The boat stopped drifting, and I found myself docked amongst some swallow weeds. I got out of the boat and then just wandered. I was tired, hungry, and thirsty. And the pain from the bite mark was excruciating. I don't think I even noticed the rocks until I fell unto them and then into the water," said Sam as he turned toward Ellie. "If your daughter wasn't there to save me, I don't think I would be here telling you or anyone my story," concluded Sam.

"I have to say you are a very lucky fellow to have faced death twice and survived," said Cy.

"After what you have been through, consider yourself a guest in our home. You are welcome to stay for as long as you need," said Ellie. "I will have Ms. Pike fix you something to eat, and you can pick a room upstairs."

"Ms. Pike!" exclaimed Daniel, unaware of her early arrival home from her vacation.

Ellie gave Daniel a wink and said, "Someone came home early. She knew this house wouldn't stay normal for very long."

Daniel smiled back in agreement and then turned to Cy. "After what Sam just told us, I am going to get a hold of my ranger friend now," said Daniel, pulling out his cell phone from his pocket.

"Agreed. Maybe he can help us track down the animal and hopefully stop any future attacks," added Cy as he and Daniel continued to strategize their next move together.

"Sam, if you are feeling strong enough, I can take you upstairs and show you around?" said Ellie, realizing the young man's well-being while under her home is now her responsibility.

"I think I can manage that. Thank you again for your hospitality," said Sam. "So, how big is this house really? And how many rooms do you have, approximately?" asked Sam as he extended his arm to Ellie in a gentlemanly fashion.

"Oh, it's pretty big. And we have a lot of rooms. It's the best 'bed and breakfast' you will ever find with the coolest amenities," laughed Ellie, graciously taking his arm and enjoying his charm.

Sam escorted Ellie to the elevator and wondered, if there was an elevator to the basement, then whatever was waiting for him upstairs, he was sure it would be something he had never seen before.

Chapter

4

The hot water rained onto my face as it washed away Sam's bloody stains that seeped through my shirt along with parts of my arms. As I stared down at the red water circling into the drain, I wondered how I was going to tell my mother about today, especially when I still couldn't understand myself. I stood under the cascading water for several uncounted minutes. I stood there recounting the day and trying to figure the *how* and the *what* and the *whys*. And the longer I stood there, the less things made any sense. I took the loofah and soaked it in bodywash then scrubbed the last remaining stains away, leaving behind a slight scent of coconut and vanilla. The steam from my shower rose up toward the ceiling and engulfed my bathroom in white mist, but I didn't care, I was stalling for time. I was not ready to face my family just yet, especially without answers. When I looked down at my fingers and saw them begin to prune, I knew hiding in here was not an option for very long. I decided to end my contemplation and turned off the water. I stepped out of the shower and reached for the towel hanging just outside my shower curtain. I also tried to make my way through a cloud of mist and blindly reached for my robe hanging on the hook by the door. Just as I was in the middle of putting on my robe, I heard the same whispering voice from the beach.

"*Go to the mirror,*" whispered the voice.

"What?" I shouted.

"*Go to the mirror,*" whispered the voice again.

I finished putting on my robe and made my way to the bathroom mirror that was covered in steam. I took my sleeve and wiped away a clearing on the glass and tried to find my reflection. I could see my outline and my dark hair slowly coming into view as the steam began to evaporate from the mirror. Finally, I saw myself looking back at me; and then suddenly, the image slowly started to change. My reflection was being replaced by a white smoky mist within the mirror. I rubbed my eyes, hoping it was a focus issue. But when I still saw the white smoky mist, I tried rubbing the mirror's front glass vigorously, thinking the steam had returned, but the mirror was dry. There was no moisture on the mirror whatsoever. I stared ahead and waited to see what was going to appear next. To my surprise, what I saw next left me speechless.

The mist began to dissipate, and as it did, I saw the outline of a woman with blond wavy hair and white milky skin. When she lifted her face to me, I saw her piercing blue eyes. That's when I knew who she was, despite only having met her once.

"Serena?" I whispered in disbelief at the reflection that was not my own.

The woman in the mirror smiled at me and then spoke. "See, I told you we would see each other again," said Serena.

"How is this happening?" I asked frantically, mesmerized by Serena's reflection.

"Emily," replied Serena, in a calming voice. "I know this may seem strange, but you have to trust me. What I am about to tell you is so very important."

"But I have so many questions, I am not sure where to start," I said, and just as I was about to utter more, Serena interrupted me.

"Yes, I know. So, let me begin to explain," replied Serena.

"Okay," I said, finally conceding and keeping my hysteria at bay for a while.

"When I gave you the gift of life, I also gave you something else. I gave you me," Serena said.

"What?" I gasped in amazement.

"You see, my magic was ending. My time was ending, so when you breathed a new breath, you also began a new life that you never knew about. I transferred my magic to you, but I had it stay dormant all these years, until now. I know you felt it, but you also never knew what it really was either," added Serena.

"So that was you all this time? And what about at the beach, was that you? Or me?" I asked, slowly coming to grips with my new reality.

"That was me awakening you. The power is within you. You healed that boy. I just showed you how," said Serena.

"That was me?" I asked.

"Yes, and there is so much more you can do," added Serena.

"Are you saying I have magic?" I asked.

"Yes, you have my magic, and as you learn and develop, it will evolve into your magic. I told you that your spirit is your strength and, together with your essence, will make this magic your own. I will be here to guide you," said Serena.

"Okay. All weirdness aside, this is amazing," I said with excitement and anticipation.

"Yes, it is a gift. But unfortunately, it does come with a price," said Serena with a bow of her head. "Emily, you are no longer mortal. You are now part of the mystic world. You will never grow old, and you will most likely outlive your family."

"Oh," I replied as my excitement turned into concern. "I remember my father having the same dilemma," I said.

"Yes, I remember. Will you be able to accept your immortality, Emily?" asked Serena with concern.

"Yes, I can accept it. But I have to know why you awakened me now after all this time?" I asked.

"That is an excellent question. There have been a series of strange events happening lately that have the potential to alter the balance of the mystic world. A very dangerous force, which has been also laid dormant and imprisoned for centuries, may be soon awakened. And if it is awakened, it will search for the items my sisters and I have guarded with our lives over the centuries," stated Serena.

"Whoa!" I exclaimed. "What would they be after? And how am I to help with this?" I asked.

"This force will be after the ancient artifacts that once belonged to Avalon's Vault," said Serena.

"Avalon's Vault?" I questioned.

"Yes, Avalon's Vault was a magnificent tomb that housed some of the most powerful magical artifacts. It stood protected by magic within the walls of a mighty fortress until the day it was destroyed," said Serena sadly.

"Fortress?" I said recalling my dreams.

"Yes, Emily, it is the same fortress you have been seeing in your dreams. When the fortress fell, the artifacts were secretly hidden to protect it from those who would use them to harm others. It was my duty to hide them, and only I know of their whereabouts," said Serena.

"So then what exactly do you want me to do?" I asked.

"You are needed to find and retrieve the artifacts, build a new vault, and become their new protector. You see, Emily, my sisters and I were known to all as the mystic sisters, but what you don't know was that we also were part of an alliance also known as the guardians of Avalon," added Serena.

"Wow, that's incredible," I said. "That's a huge responsibility," I added, coming to realize the severity of the task.

"Yes, I realize that. And I know it is going to be great task for you," said Serena.

"I see that," I said, nodding. "And I know I will need my family's help. So then all I need is for you to tell them everything you told me. So they don't think I am going crazy cause, this will be hard for them to swallow. And they will all think I am losing my mind," I added with a chuckle.

"Well, that is going to be a bit more complicated," said Serena with a melancholic look.

"What do you mean?" I asked.

"Emily, you are the only one I can speak to and the only one who can see me. Remember, I am inside you. And the only way we can communicate is through your reflection," added Serena.

"Aah, nuts! There had to be a catch, huh?" I said, wondering how I am ever going to explain this to my family.

"Emily, I must go now," said Serena as her image began to diminish.

"Wait! There is so much more I need to know. What do I do if I need to contact you?" I asked,

Serena's image slightly faded back. "Just find your reflection and call out my name," said Serena as her image completely disappeared and my reflection slowly faded out of focus within the mirror.

I was too distracted by the look of my wet stringy hair that I hadn't noticed the voice behind me.

"Emily! Who were you talking to?" asked Ms. Pike, standing by my bathroom door.

Completely startled, I jumped and turned around, holding my chest. "Ms. Pike, you scared me. I didn't hear you come in," I said, still holding my chest.

"Well, I would assume you wouldn't since you seemed so involved in what sounded like a conversation," said Ms. Pike as she looked around my bathroom and found no one with me. "So, who were you talking to?" Ms. Pike asked again.

"Um, I- I..." I stuttered, then finally confessed. "I was talking to myself. I was trying to piece together today events and didn't realize I was talking out loud," I added, hoping Ms. Pike would believe me.

"Oh, okay, if you say so, dear," said Ms. Pike with a shrug. "Anyways, your mother asked me to check on you while I was upstairs, getting settled in my room."

"Wait, you are home early from your vacation, why?" I asked, walking out of the bathroom and into my bedroom.

"Yes, I am," said Ms. Pike as she followed me to my bedroom and sat on my bed.

"I thought you were having a great time. You had the sun and the sand," I said, moving in and out of my closet, finding clothes to wear.

"Oh, you know me, dear. I find it hard to stay away too long. Besides, when I walked in, I ran into your mother, and she filled me in on the latest goings-on in this house. I sense a new adventure is brewing," said Ms. Pike with a wink.

"Ahh, nothing gets by you," I said, finding a spot next to Ms. Pike on my bed.

"Are you okay, dear?" asked Ms. Pike with concern.

I looked at Ms. Pike's worried eyes, and I couldn't lie to her, "All I can say is that there is something new about me, and it's big—I mean, huge news. Almost unbelievable news, but in all fairness, it's going to have to be said to everyone in the family, all at once. I'm just not sure how exactly without Mom or Father thinking I am off my rocker," I said.

"Oh, I see—that kind of news. Well then, I'm sure you will find a way, dear," said Ms. Pike as she cupped my hand between both hers. "Don't fret, you have never disappointed us before," added Ms. Pike.

"I'm glad you came home," I said with a smile, followed by a wrapping hug.

"Hahaha," laughed Ms. Pike. "Emily, I will always be here for you, your father, and your mother. You can never get rid of little old me," said Ms. Pike. "Now, I must tend to the kitchen. I have a feeling there are stomachs rumbling about this place," added Ms. Pike as she rose from my bed, kissed my forehand, and made her way downstairs. "I will let your mother know you will be down shortly," hollered Ms. Pike, from the hallway.

"Thank you," I hollered back.

With the clothes I had chosen to wear in hand, I finished getting ready. As I dressed myself, putting on each item one at a time, I wondered how I was going to explain Serena. *If I am the only one who can talk to her and see her, then how will everyone know I am telling the truth?* I thought. *And without everyone on board, I can't search for the artifacts, and how am I going to build a vault?* Distracted by my Serena thoughts, I suddenly remembered the reason I was in the shower in the first place. *Sam,* I thought.

Chapter

5

Ellie had just finished giving Sam a tour of the library after their walk-through of the main level of the mansion. Before heading upstairs to find Sam a bedroom for the night, Sam's growling stomach and Ellie's prenatal need for a snack led them to another area of the house: the kitchen. Sam's eyes widened in amazement as it did with all the "first-time room entrances" in the house. But his astonishment of the kitchen went far beyond the other rooms. The solid wooden cabinets stood from floor to ceiling, and the shelves made of the same wooden finish filled the room with the smell of cedar. In the middle stood the longest island Sam had ever seen, it had a dark-brown smooth granite top that sat upon a base that was made of brick, reddish brown in color. The cushioned seats to the island were made of the same brick design. Sam sat at one and counted the chairs. The final total were twelve seats all arranged on one side of the table. He wondered why there were no flat TV screens on the walls around since nowadays, most kitchens had them. It was not until he placed his elbows on the granite top that he noticed, built into the island top, were two touch-screen TVs. As Sam swiveled around his chair, he saw that on the south side of the wall looked to be the cooking area. The back splash was all brick and stone while the gas stove ran from one end of the wall to the other. And tucked at the end was a large wooden stove with giant pipes leading up to the roof. Sam went to touch the fridge door and noticed there were in fact three doors to the fridge. While trying to find the doorknob to open the middle fridge door, Sam noticed the black smooth fridge door illuminate; and as if looking through a window, Sam saw all the items in the fridge without even opening it. He proceeded to touch the next fridge door, revealing the same windowlike feature behind fridge door number 2 and so on with fridge door number 3. The kitchen had a rustic feel as soon as you walked in, but it was the appliances that made Sam question to himself, *How technologically advance is this place?*

"Pretty cool, huh?" asked Ellie, already snacking on an apple.

"Um, this is way beyond cool. It's over the top, whoa!" said Sam with enthusiasm.

Ellie laughed. "My daughter, Emily, thought the same thing when she first got here too. But after a while, you get use to the grandeur of this place," said Ellie.

"I have never seen a place like this before. There is nothing like this where I come from," said Sam.

"If you think this is something, you should see the castle," said Ms. Pike, in an excited tone.

"Ms. Pike, this is Sam," said Ellie, making the introduction.

"Hello, young man. Nice to see you are off the gurney and alive," said Ms. Pike, extending her hand for a greeting.

"Nice to meet you. And yes, I am very grateful for being alive. And I still have not had the chance to properly thank my savior yet," said Sam.

"Where is Emily anyways? I thought she would be down by now," said Ellie.

"Oh, I chatted with her upstairs. She will be down momentarily. In the meantime, who's hungry?" said Ms. Pike, wrapping her apron around her waist.

"Starved!" said Sam.

"Just give me a few minutes, and I will have something whipped up for you in a jiffy," said Ms. Pike.

"Please, you don't need to go through too much trouble," said Sam.

"Oh, pish-posh, it's no trouble at all. Just make yourself comfy on the island," said Ms. Pike as she began to work her culinary magic by the cooking area.

Ellie climbed onto one of the chairs next to Sam, lifting to the table a piece of pumpkin pie and a spray can of whipped cream. "Ms. Pike is right. Get comfy, she will take care of you. Like she takes care of all of us," said Ellie, spraying the can of whip cream onto her pie.

"Looks like you're really hungry," said Sam.

"I'm eating for two, remember?" said Ellie, scooping a piece of pie plus whipped cream into her mouth.

"Duly noted. How far along are you?" asked Sam.

"Far along to know I'm ready to have this baby now. But really, I'm about eight and a half months," said Ellie, holding her belly.

"Then please continue to feed your unborn offspring. Oh, and by the way, what castle?" asked Sam eagerly. To feed Sam's curiosity, Ellie proceeded to tell Sam about the castle in England.

—m—

As I made my way to the lower level, an aroma so tasty caught my attention. Instead of heading to Cy's lab as I had planned, I made a slight detour to see what was cooking in the kitchen.

"Yum, I can smell whatever you are cooking from the stairs, Ms. Pike," I said.

"Emily, there you are," said my mother, nearly finishing her pie.

"Mom! Enjoying your pie, I see," I said, with a smirk.

"Of course! Sam, this is my daughter, Emily," said my mother.

"Hi! It's nice to finally meet you," said Sam, rising from the island and extending his hand toward mine.

"Sam? You're alive and breathing and walking," I said, surprised, eager to extend my hand to meet his.

"Yeah, when we first met, I was not at my best," said Sam.

"Yeah, you were slightly unconscious," I said with a laugh.

Sam laughed, "You could say that."

"I'm glad you are actually up and around," I said, taking a seat by the island.

"If it wasn't for you and Cy, I don't think I would be anything right now," said Sam, finding a seat next to me.

"Please, I just happened to be at the right place at the right time," I said, trying to avoid adding more to the conversation.

"Oh, I think you did more, from what I hear," said my mother, turning toward me and giving the "I know more than you think" look.

"Oh, what do you mean by that?" I asked, testing to see how much my mother did know.

"Well, Sam told us something about you possibly healing him. Do you have an explanation for that?" asked my mother with persistence.

"Actually, I do now have an explanation for that. But I think it is best I tell everyone all together," I said.

"Come and get 'em! Soups on," interrupted Ms. Pike as she filled the island with a plate of sliced chicken breasts on a bed of penne noodles topped with Alfredo sauce. And also, a plate of steamed garlic-butter broccolini and crusty bread twists stuffed with mozzarella cheese.

"This looks so good!" said Sam, rubbing his hands together, ready to dive into the meal.

"I agree. I'm hungry too," I added. "Sorry, Mom, the explanation will have to wait. Food is a-calling, and my tummy is a-rumbling," I said, reaching for the grub placed before me.

—✲—

Ellie watched as the youngsters devoured their meals and started to enjoy each other's company. She knew she had to wait for her answers. She trusted her daughter, but somehow, Ellie could not shake the feeling that what Emily had to tell them was not going to be what she wanted to hear, or expect to hear. She looked down at her protruding belly and feared that whatever path that was about to present itself, she would not be able to be a part of. Ellie looked back at her daughter and Sam and smiled. There was also something happening between these two, she could feel it. There was a reason fate brought these two individuals together, like there was a reason she and Daniel were brought together all those years ago, thought Ellie. Yet until the reason decided to manifest, she knew she would need patience and maybe a great deal of faith to get through it.

Chapter

6

Daniel paced the floor in Cy's lab, talking on his phone to his park ranger contact while Cy was creating a three-dimensional layout of the forest over the Brain Table.

"That's perfect, thanks again, Rick. We will see you tomorrow," said Daniel to the voice on his phone.

"What did your ranger friend have to say?" asked Cy.

"Rick said he had noticed some fresh larger-than-usual animal tracks in some areas of the woods. But he hadn't heard of any attacks made on any of campers or hikers yet. He did say he would meet us tomorrow afternoon at the ranger station and then lead us to where he found the tracks," said Daniel.

"Okay, that is start. I also think it would be a good idea to bring Sam along, being the only one who encountered the animal," said Cy.

"I agree. It will take us a couple hours to get to the ranger's station though. I am thinking it would be best to get an early start. We should prepare the camping gear as well," said Daniel.

"Okay, and just so I'm clear, this is a catch-and-cage mission, right?" added Cy.

"Yes! If there is a large animal running wild, then we will need to find it. And if the animal is as big as Sam says, then we will need some of your best DES equipment specifically designed to cage and transport if needed," said Daniel.

"I see, well, since we may be camping and carrying hunting equipment, I recently finished working on some lightweight camping gear that I packed in the storage room. And this item would be perfect for the hunting aspect," said Cy, pulling from one of his workbenches a utility belt handymen would wear around their waist, just smaller in size.

"What do you have there?" asked Daniel, with curiosity.

"This is a military-grade utility belt. It's lightweight and fitted with some of my ingenious DES goodies yet." Cy smiled, giving it to Daniel to observe up close.

"This is really lightweight, wow! Now, tell me about the goodies," asked Daniel.

"Well, in these slots are the tranquilizer bullets. And in this square pocket is our caging device," said Cy, pointing to specific areas on the belt.

"So where is the gun for the bullets?" asked Daniel as he reached inside the square pocket for the caging device.

"Ah well, I designed these bullets so we don't need guns to release them. We just need to throw them at the target. You see, I have been experimenting with nano-bot programming, and these little gems are my prototypes," said Cy, holding a slim two-inch bullet-type object in his hand.

"Cy, there are no pointy edges to these bullets, how's it going to puncture the animal?" asked Daniel.

"What you see it just the casing, like you would find in any bullet. Once the bullet is airborne, the nano-bots are programmed to open the casing and reshape the bullet to reveal its pointed end. It's also programmed to propel the bullet toward its target with even more velocity until it actually reaches its target," said Cy.

"So, it's basically a miniature heat-sinking missile?" laughed Daniel

"Exactly, like that. Once the bullet has hit its target, the tranquillizer will first attack the animal limbs. The animal will experience a numbing feeling in their legs, rendering them immobile," stated Cy.

"Very, nice! Okay, and now, explain this," asked Daniel, holding up two tiny flat disks he found in the square pockets.

"Yes, okay, so once the animal has fallen to the ground, the disks are released in pairs in the air as well. The disks are also designed with nanotechnology that are programmed to create an invisible cage around the animal. What's interesting about this cage is that it can levitate the animal without any one of us having to get close to it to move it," said Cy.

"Brilliant. And what is this? It looks like the garage door opener?" asked Daniel, picking up the object clipped to the belt.

"Oh, that really is our garage door opener—well…*was* anyways." said Cy. "I needed the casing because I had an idea for something. I am still working out the bugs, but I think I almost have it figured out. This little device will most likely be kept on my belt instead of yours."

"Mine?" asked Daniel.

"I made two on the assumption you and I would both be wearing them. Besides, when have you ever known me to not plan for all contingences?" said Cy.

"Cy, after all these years of working together, I assure you I never doubt your planning skills. I trust it, like I trust my own beating heart. It's just automatic," said Daniel.

Cy looked at his long-time friend and, with a smirk, continued to work on the garage door opener device at his workbench.

Daniel laid the utility belt on Cy's table. "While you finish up here, Cy, I will find Emily and get her to help me round up the camping gear from the storage room," said Daniel.

"Sounds good to me. Everything I am working on should be ready for tomorrow," said Cy, lifting his head from his bench.

"Good. Let's plan to leave early morning for the ranger station," said Daniel toward Cy, who now was completely engaged in his work that the only reply he could muster was a low grunt. Daniel nodded his head in acceptance and headed upstairs to find the others.

Daniel made his way up the elevator to the main level. Once the elevator doors opened, Daniel knew what direction to go toward to find the others. All he had to do was follow the smell of cooked food and the rumbling of his stomach. There were two human qualities he had missed enjoying during his vampire days, the taste and smell of food. He knew now tasting food and smelling it were far beyond the satisfaction of blood. The purpose of blood for him then was used to satisfy a hunger and restore strength to his body. Now, as a mortal, he can experience cravings and savor the taste of food, a variety of food. As Daniel drew closer to the kitchen, not only did the smell of food grab his attention but also did the sound of laughter and conversation.

—⁓—

"Seriously, a vampire?" said Sam, reacting to my story about my encounter with Gideon.

"Yes, a very nasty one. Now, pass the plate of broccolini," I said.

"I'm starting to understand that this household is not like any normal household," said Sam, laying the plate before my reach.

"You can say that. Now that you have heard about Emily's story about Gideon and Ellie's reveal of the castle, why are you not running for the door?" questioned Ms. Pike.

Sam laughed, "Well, my grandfather always told me there is a constant battle between good and evil in this world. I always believed that evil could come in any shape or form. And his brother was a spellcaster too. So, at a very young age, the spirit world and the reality of magic were more than just bedtime stories to me," said Sam.

"Magic? You believe in magic?" I asked with a curious look.

"Yes! I believe that there is a force far beyond our normal existence. I was taught that everything living has an energy force. And people like my grandfather's brother had the ability to tap into it, draw it out, and transform it," said Sam, "So, whatever you did for me on the beach, Emily, I am not afraid of it. I'm truly grateful. And I assure you, I will never ask any questions, nor will I ever need any explanations," added Sam.

I looked at Sam with such gratitude, and even though I knew the questions Sam would never ask, I now had answers for. I was comforted by Sam's acknowledgement and acceptance. For the first time, I had a glimpse of what it would feel like to have someone, aside from my family, I could confide in, trust, and maybe reveal my true self without judgement and without fear. *How far could I trust Sam?* I wondered.

I watched my father enter the kitchen and find his way to my mother's side. They looked so happy together wrapped in each other's arms, I thought. It was at that moment I decided to tell them everything I had recently come to know. I had to do it now while I had the courage.

"So, who wants to know the truth about what happened on the beach and with Sam?" I said, clearing my throat, hoping to get the attention of everyone in the room.

I looked around at the faces that now all turned toward my direction, so I continued, "Everyone might want to take a seat for this," I said.

Just as I was about to jump into my story, Sam's hand started to slowly raise into the air.

"Did you want me to leave the room for this?" he asked in a meek tone.

I smiled. "No, Sam. Please stay. You need to hear this too."

"Oh, take a seat, dearie, I have been waiting to hear this," said Ms. Pike, quickly moving away from the stove and finding the closest seat by the island.

"You have our attention, honey, go ahead," said my mother.

"Okay, I think the best way to explain this is to start from the very beginning. I mean three years to be accurate when we were in the caverns," I said.

"What happened in the caverns?" asked Sam curiously.

Ms. Pike turned to Sam to help bring clarity, "Three years ago, Gideon killed Emily. She died and then was brought back to life by a sorceress named Serena. Continue, dear," said Ms. Pike, offering a quick summary, allowing me to move on with my explanation.

Sam gave a slight nod and focused his attention back to me.

"Thanks, Ms. Pike," I said. "So when Serena brought me back, she did more than just give me my life back. Serena knew her time was coming to an end, therefore, she decided to give me another gift but never told me about it. For years, it was kept hidden until I met Sam and saved his life," I said.

"What was the gift?" asked my mother.

"Serena gave me her magic," I said.

"What? How?" my mother questioned.

"Wait, Serena's magic was always through touch," added my father.

"Yes, it was. And now, her magic is mine. When I touched Sam's wounds and healed them, it was with Serena's guidance. She told me that was the moment she awakened the magic within me. Magic saved you, Sam. Magic that came from inside me," I said, hoping he would stay true to his convictions and not run or be afraid of me.

"Cool," said Sam with a smile.

Relieved to see Sam still seated and still interested in more of what I had to say, I continued to explain more about Serena.

"Serena told me the reason why she awakened me. The primary reason was that there is something coming—if not already here— and it will be after the artifacts from Avalon's Vault. Serena was a former guardian and protector of these artifacts as well as one of the mystic sisters. She told me what used to be her responsibility is now my responsibility. She wants me to find the artifacts and house them in a new vault to protect them," I explained.

"I can confirm that Serena was one of the mystic sisters. And, she did tell me once that she was the guardian of the book of Mystics. I just always thought Avalon's Vault was just a legend," my father added.

"Apparently, everything you have said Daniel seems to back up what Emily is saying," said Ms. Pike.

"Emily, how long have you known about your new path?" my mother asked me.

"I sort of just found out," I said, realizing how crazy my words were sounding.

"Are you saying Serena was here and told you all this?" asked my father.

"Kind of," I said, hesitating for a moment.

"So, where is she? Have her tell us her side," said my mother, still trying to process.

"This is where things are going to get a bit complicated. And I will need you to keep an open mind about this. So, remember when I said Serena's time was ending? That meant her physical self too. So honestly, she does not exist anymore, except inside me," I said.

"So, how does she talk to you?" asked my father.

"Well, at first I was hearing her voice in my head. And then she appeared to me in a different way," I said.

"Dear, was that whom you were talking to in the bathroom?" asked Ms. Pike.

"Yes. I'm sorry for lying to you. But I was not sure how to explain myself at that moment," I said.

"Bathroom? How did she appear to you in the bathroom?" asked my mother.

"I think I know how. You saw Serena through your own reflection, right?" said Sam out loud.

"Yes!" I said, "She led me to the mirror and then she appeared. This is how I can communicate with her, but only I can communicate with her. No one else can."

"My grandfather used to say that one's reflection can hold a great deal of power. He used to describe it as a portal," said Sam.

"Sam is right. The mystic world often uses a person's reflection as a vehicle to communicate with another soul or dimension," added my father.

I looked around the kitchen at everyone's faces to gauge how much everyone had digested my story. From what I can tell, Ms. Pike and Sam seemed to be the only ones excited about what I had to say. My father was intrigued but my mother, on the other hand, had her motherly concerns. It was at that moment I decided against sharing the new truth about my mortality, for now anyways.

"Emily, I do believe you. But you must understand this is really a lot to take in without proof. I just wish Serena was here, so she can speak on this too. I know Serena, and if I just saw her, I would be more convinced of the urgency of your new responsibility," said my father.

"Sorry, honey, I agree with your father. We just need more details," added my mother.

"We are just in the middle of planning to track down the wolf that bit Sam," said my father.

"You were bitten by a wolf?" I asked Sam, recalling the bite mark I found.

"Yes, in the woods before you found me. It was huge. Your father and Cy think it will cause more harm to others if it's still alive. We still are not sure of that though," said Sam, turning his comment to my father.

"True, but my ranger friend did say he found fresh tracks in some areas. So, we are going on the assumption the animal might have survived the fall into the rapids. We made plans to meet him tomorrow. Sam, Cy and I agree you should come too," said my father.

"Sure, count me in," said Sam, with excitement.

"Emily, you up for it too?" my father asked me.

"Of course!" I said. "And in all fairness, we can come back to the Serena thing when we get back. I agree with you all, we need to know more. And Serena ended our conversation sooner than I wanted, before I could get more information. My goal was to at least fill you all in on what I found out. We will need Serena to somehow continue to explain, when and if we can figure out how everyone is able to see and hear what I can," I added.

"Yeah, you mean somehow mind-meld with you," said Sam with a smirk.

"Exactly!" I said, in agreement.

"I agree, first thing is first. We will find out more about Sam's animal attack and then sort out your new responsibility, Emily. Now, help me get the camping gear from the storage before it gets too late. We have an early day tomorrow," said my father.

Before following to help Sam and my father, I had caught the concerned look my mother gave to my father and then her glance over to me. "Emily, I realize this must be so strange for you. And I cannot help but worry more about you now," said my mother.

"I see this is going to be hard for you to imagine much less understand because I know I barely am comprehending all this myself. But if there is one thing you have always taught me was to follow my gut and trust my instincts," I said.

"And what is your gut telling you about what Serena told you?" asked my mother.

"My gut is telling me to not be afraid. For months, I could feel there was something inside me just waiting to come out, and I didn't know what it was until now. It was magic, Mom. Magic that was hidden deep inside me and magic that was given as a gift. I have to honor this gift," I said.

My mother looked at me and cradled my face with her hands. "You are the gift. You are my gift. And I am so proud to have you as my daughter. And when your new brother or sister inside me finally comes into this world, they too will know how wonderful their big sister truly is," said my mother.

I smiled and wrapped my arms around my mother, giving her a big hug. I could sense she had found clarity in my answer.

And as I left her embrace, she watched me walk down the hall to join Sam and my father.

I have to trust her and let go, Ellie thought.

Chapter

7

Deep within the forest, still lost and lying on a small green patch of grass was the indigo-blue wine-shaped bottle that slipped from Sam's fingers. It was finally free from its magical wooden-box prison. The magic that kept the lock impenetrable over the centuries was somehow broken. And the box that encased it was shattered into pieces. The bottle went unnoticed for hours by many. Those who glanced at it mistook it for trash and just simply walked away. One spectator raised the bottle from its resting place and noticed it was still corked. After many failed attempts to uncork the bottle and shatter the glass, the bottle was once again discarded to the ground, like trash. The bottle braved the elements of the sunlight during day and the cold and dampness of the night. Yet unknown to all, no ordinary person could release the cork. The cork was guarded by a very powerful spell. A spell that was the last line of defense should the bottle be found. There was a reason why the lock, the box, and the cork were protected by magic; whatever was inside the bottle was meant to stay inside the bottle. However, nothing ever stays as it should be forever as a pair of hiking boots straddled over the bottle and a pair of man's hands reached down to pick up the hourglass object from the grass. A bearded man in a plaid shirt lifted the bottle to his face and rubbed some of the dirt off to create a clean patch to look inside. When the man noticed the bottle was empty, he also had the urge to leave it behind but decided against it. Instead, the bottle was packed into his bag. The bearded man trekked back through the woods as if he knew the area very well. He walked alone through the bush and tall trees. The sun was able to peek through some of the leaves from trees, providing some warmth to the lower-lying grass and plant life. But the chill of the air and the lack of warmth didn't concern the bearded man as he walked with only his plaid shirt on. For countless months that had turned into years, he hadn't felt the cold on his body or on his face. He was constantly warm, almost as if his body temperature had its own furnace that radiated within him daily. The daytime was the only period the bearded man felt and could be normal—human, you could say. As he reached the edge of the woods to a familiar clearing, he looked down at his watch and noticed the time. He calculated the hours left before nightfall and quickened his pace. The goal was to reach his cabin before dusk. And even though he knew his way about the woods, he also knew that he did not want to be in these woods during the night. He was afraid for himself and for others should that ever happen again. As planned, he reached his small cabin where he lived alone. The cabin was all log in structure, very rustic and cozy from the outside. The bearded man opened his door and walked inside. He laid his bag on the table and removed its contents. The indigo-blue bottle was taken out of the bag and laid onto the table among other items. Just as he was about to head toward the basement for his usual nightly routine, the cell phone he placed on the table began to ring. The bearded man answered the call and greeted the familiar man's voice on the other end. The two men talked for a few minutes and agreed to a meeting tomorrow. The evening sky was drawing near, so the bearded man hurried to the basement before the moon took its place among the stars. The staircase to the basement was winding and narrow. It led the man down to the lowest level of the cabin, as if walking into a dungeon; the bearded man came to his nightly resting place. He walked through the iron bars and closed the steel cage door behind him and took off his shirt. On the wall were two iron shackles he fastened tightly to his wrists and one big wide one he clamped onto his waist. The bearded man was securely bonded as the moon rose into the night sky and shone through a small window of the cell. Day after day, month after month, and year after year, this was the nightly routine;

as the day slowly transformed into night, the bearded man transformed from a human into an animal.

Sam and I finished loading the last of the camping gear with my father. The gear was separated into four packs for each of us to carry. My father lifted the last pack into the Jeep we were going to take to the ranger's station.

"Okay, that should do it," said my father, securing the last piece to the Jeep's roof.

"Great, I am actually really tired," said Sam.

"As you should be, considering you had a very eventful last couple days," said my father. "Emily, why don't you help Sam get set up with a room upstairs," he added.

"Sure thing," I said. "Come on, Sam. You can choose whatever room you want," I added, leading Sam back to house.

"Remember you two, we leave at 8:00 a.m., so get some sleep," shouted my father.

Sam and I waved in acknowledgement and then disappeared up the staircase.

"How many rooms do I get to choose from?" asked Sam.

"Well," I said, leading him up the stairs, "I'll just have to show you."

I led Sam up the stairs and to the east wing of the upper level. As we came to the beginning of the hallway, I pointed to a long stretch of doors. "Take your pick," I said.

Sam looked down the hall to a series of reddish-brown closed doors. "Are all these rooms not being used?" Sam asked in awe.

"This is our guest wing of the house. There were about seven to eight rooms down this hall and about two or three around the corner. These rooms here, the ones around the corner and closer to the staircase, have their own bathrooms," I added.

"Oh, I'm definitely liking my own bathroom," said Sam, heading toward around the corner.

Sam opened the first door closest to the staircase and walked inside. The room was similar to a suite in a hotel room, yet with more of a homey touch and feel. He plopped himself onto the king-sized bed and came to conclusion there was no more choices to make. He was happy where he was.

"Are you sure you don't care to see any other rooms," I asked, laughing at Sam's seemingly lifeless body lying on the bed.

"Oh, I'm sure. If the other rooms are just like this, then there is no point. Besides, I am completely exhausted, I don't think I have the motivation right now to go room exploring. I have never felt this tired in my life. Your dad is probably right, these past couple of days have been more than usual for me. I think all I need is a good-night's sleep, and then I should be ready to go tomorrow," said Sam.

"That's sounds like a good plan," I said. "If you need anything, my room is just down the hall in the east wing, which is opposite the guest wing. Or just in case you get lost, hang a left from your door," I added.

"Okay, thanks," said Sam with a smirk. "Hey, Emily, is your family always like this?"

"What do you mean?" I asked, just about to cross the door threshold.

"I mean, they don't know me, and they have been very kind and welcoming," said Sam.

"Well, first off, you didn't head for the door once you awoke in Cy's lab, and second, you didn't run away when I told you about me. And in this household, acceptance of the abnormal or the unusual is the standard. Basically, you fit right in. Plus, my family has this knack for helping those in need. It's like a reflex," I said.

Sam chuckled. "Okay, fair enough. So, about your newfound magic, how do you really feel about it?" asked Sam.

"It's hard to explain, but I think the best way to describe it is like being on pause. I know I must move forward, but right now, I can't because I have my doubts about my abilities. I know how I felt when I healed you on the beach, but I don't understand how my magic works. Serena keeps telling me I have all this power, but I am still unsure how to use it," I said.

"I think in time you will figure it all out. Your family is your support system, among other things. I only had my grandfather. He was my rock and my protector. Without him, I think I would have turned out very differently," said Sam.

"Had? Isn't your grandfather back home? He must be worried about you," I said.

"Um, he passed away about a month ago," said Sam.

"I'm sorry to hear that. How did he pass?" I asked, walking back toward Sam's bed.

"My grandfather just went to bed one night and never awoke the next morning. The coroner said it was heart failure. The stink about all of it was that I was the one that found him the next morning. That was the first time since I lost my parents that I felt so helpless. When I finished all the funeral arrangements, I knew I couldn't stay, so I left and have been travelling ever since," said Sam, staring at the floor, not able to look up.

"Hey," I said, trying to meet Sam's eyes. "You are not alone anymore. You might be surrounded by kooks and odd characters, but that's what makes our family so unique. We will always have your back no matter what. Family means loyalty, and loyalty in this family is forever," I said.

Sam looked up at me. "You know, for the first time in weeks, I am feeling something so familiar. Something I thought I somehow lost over the years. It is a feeling I had not felt since I was young and when my parents were alive," confessed Sam.

"Oh, and what is that?" I asked.

"It's the feeling of home. I feel at home with you, Emily, in this mansion, and at home with these new people I never imagined ever being in my world," said Sam.

I smiled at Sam, feeling grateful for sharing. "You're stuck with us now. Get some sleep. We have an early day tomorrow," I said, moving back toward the door.

"Yeah, right. Don't let the door hit you on the way out!" said Sam jokingly.

I gave a slight smirk and proceeded to walk into the hallway. I understood Sam, and in return, Sam was beginning to understand me.

As Emily left the room, her footsteps faded down the hallway. Sam looked around at his huge room and noticed some extra clothes laid out for him by the dresser. There were three piles laid out, and as he drew closer to them, he saw a note next to the last pile, which read, *From the best B&B you will ever find.*

Sam laughed. He knew it came from Ellie and thought how comforting it was to feel looked after, but how did Ellie know he would be in this room? He shrugged off the thought and reached for the pile that seemed to have what looked like pajamas for the night. He then packed the other piles of clothing into a duffle bag that coincidentally happened to be nicely placed on the floor next to the dresser. *Wow, she really thinks of everything*, Sam thought still smiling.

Sam changed into the pajama pants and decided to forgo the shirt. He found the room warmer than usual, or was it he that was feeling warmer than usual? Sam couldn't tell, nor did he care. Instead, he just wanted to climb between the sheets and get settled in for a good-night's sleep.

After several minutes, the rest Sam had hoped to find became elusive. He was restless and growing warm. He could feel his body get hot. He threw the sheets off the bed and leaped off onto the floor, heading toward the window. Sam cranked the small knob to open the glass frame. The night breeze was cool, almost chilly for some; but to Sam, it brought comfort to his stifling room. Sam stood by the window, shirtless, breathing in the cold air. The night air was crisp and had the same smell as it did during his many campouts. But, tonight felt odd. Sam wiped his brow and noticed the small beads of sweat that formed there. He looked down at his chest and could see the same happening there as well. *How could I be sweating in this cold air?* he thought.

Sam moved to a larger handle and cranked it, opening an even larger window. The larger window not only allowed the winds from the night air to blow into his room, making the curtains sway back, but also it allowed the moon's light to beam directly into Sam's room. The moon was calling Sam. When Sam looked up at the bright halo in the sky, something surged inside him. Suddenly, an incredible pain from Sam's abdomen caused him to drop to the floor. Sam crouched on his knees, holding his stomach as his spine began to pulse, almost as if it was going to break open. The pain came in waves, like contractions that lasted several seconds until another wave would come. When he felt one of the pain waves subside, Sam rose to his feet and made his way to the bed, away from the window and the moonlight. Lying in bed, he pulled the covers over his body, hoping to shield him from whatever was happening. However, whatever was happening already had begun its course. And although Sam lay hidden from the moonlight, he could feel himself changing beneath the sheets. An uncontrollable rage started to build within him. He tried to ignore it, but it was slowly consuming him. Sam was convinced he would not let himself succumb to these emotions, these primal rages. He would fight until he couldn't. Then as he came to the edge of winning tonight's battle, Sam uncontrollably yet instinctively let out a low animal growl beneath his covers. The transformation stopped; Sam became Sam again, but for how long, he did not know.

Chapter

8

Dawn had arrived. Everyone in the mansion was already up and busily moving about, except for Sam. Cy loaded his equipment onto the Jeep and headed for the kitchen for a chance at Ms. Pike's early morning continental breakfast spread. The rest of the group finished what they needed to do and then headed toward the kitchen for a bite before departing. My father, mother, and I each entered the kitchen to find Cy already seated at the island, enjoying his meal. Ms. Pike watched as each member visited the buffet table and took a seat at the island. With a curious look, she wondered why there was one member still missing.

"Where is our new guest?" asked Ms. Pike, referring to Sam.

"I'm sure he is still getting ready. What a slowpoke," I said.

"Well, I hope he gets himself ready quickly, or he won't get a chance to eat," added my mother.

"We will give him five more minutes and then we will go up get him," said my father.

"He was pretty tired when I left him last night," I said, realizing that since speaking with Serena, my nightly dreams ended. I had finally slept like a baby throughout the night.

"Maybe he just needed to hit the snooze button a few more times this morning," Cy added.

"Okay, well, time's up. I'll go get him," said my father, rising from his seat.

Just as my father was about to leave his seat, Sam casually entered the kitchen.

"We thought you slept in," said my mother.

"Almost, I kind of abused the snooze button on my alarm this morning," said Sam, scratching his head.

Cy laughed, "See, I told you."

"How did you sleep?" my mother asked.

Sam hesitated. "I slept okay. Had a hard time at the beginning, but then eventually, I tired myself out. Ellie, thank you for the clothes, by the way," said Sam, trying to divert from any more sleeping questions.

"You're welcome!" replied my mother.

"How did you know I was going to choose that room out of the others?" Sam asked her.

"Well, it was the one closest to the stairs, had its own bathroom, and I knew you were tired. Call it a gut feeling," said my mother with an all-knowing motherly smile.

"I'm still not used to all this," Sam said.

"All what?" my mother asked.

"Someone looking out for me," Sam replied.

"You're stuck with us now. So get used to it," said my mother.

Sam smiled and whispered under his breath, "Like mother, like daughter."

As Sam made his way to the breakfast station, he glanced in Emily's direction just as she was clearing her plate.

Sam thought, *Emily should know about what happened last night, she would be the only one who would maybe understand even if I couldn't comprehend myself what was going on. But now was not the time."*

Sam smiled and whispered under his breath, "Like mother, like daughter."

I waved at Sam and motioned him to meet me by the Jeep when he finished filling his plate.

"Sam, you might want to take your food to go because we need to start heading out," said my father, motioning everyone to head toward the door.

"Here, dear," said Ms. Pike, handing Sam a take-out container. "Daniel has always been the stern, punctual type. Best not make him wait," Ms. Pike added with a smile.

"Thank you, Ms. Pike, but I don't think I will need the take-out container, just a few napkins," said Sam as he managed to stack the food into one giant breakfast sandwich.

Ms. Pike chuckled at Sam's clever breakfast solution and handed him a large cloth napkin to wrap his sandwich in. Sam scooped up a small bottle of juice from the station and tucked it into his backpack for later. Heading toward the door, he carried with him his large breakfast sandwich in one hand and a carton of milk in the other. Sam once again thanked Ms. Pike for her kindness and hurried to rejoin us, who were now all gathered outside by the Jeep.

Cy had already made his way to the passenger's side of the Jeep and began programming the route on the GPS device. As Sam made his way down the front step, he saw me standing by the Jeep's door.

"You are quite the slowpoke this morning," I said.

"I know. I'm sorry. I guess last night wasn't as restful as I hoped," Sam said.

"Are you okay?" I asked, noticing how tired Sam looked.

"There is something I need to tell you. Just not now. I'll tell you later," said Sam. "After my breakfast," he added, lifting his sandwich to my face and taking a bite.

"Okay, I will hold you to that," I said following Sam into the back seat of the Jeep and closing the door.

My mother approached the back-passenger window of the Jeep. "Be careful. And take care of each other," my mother said.

My father followed behind her and wrapped his arms around her shoulders. "We will. We always do," said father.

"Daniel, be safe, and you too, Emily," said my mother with concern. "I wish I could be there with you all," she added.

"Don't worry, Mother. We will be back soon," I said with reassurance.

"It's going to be a simple catch and cage," said Cy. "We got this," Cy added.

"That is all good. But I would feel more at ease if you also had this with you as well," Mom said, pulling out a long phone device from her pocket and handing it to my father.

My father looked down at the device and smirked. "The satellite phone," he said as he leaned in and gave Mom a hug followed by a tender kiss.

"See you soon," he whispered softly.

My father then walked to the other side of the Jeep, climbed into the driver's seat, and fired up the engine.

As the Jeep drove down the driveway and away from the mansion, I looked back and watched my mother wave good-bye. I knew how much my mother would have wanted to be with us. I also knew how much more she would worry about us too, especially since my father no longer had his vampire abilities. Before, she trusted in the knowledge that nothing could harm us. But now, it was different. In her mind, we were all vulnerable to anything. I shared some of my mother's fear despite the truth about my own new mortality. *Am I ready to be the protector Serena wants me to be?* I thought.

Drifting further into more of my thoughts, I had remembered what Sam said. *What did he have to tell me?* I wondered.

I looked over at my backseat companion and noticed he had drifted off to sleep. I suppose he needed to catch up on the rest he missed out on last night. I pulled out my headphones and decided to listen to some music. As I was about to activate my screen, I heard a voice whisper my name. I knew it was Serena calling me, but I didn't know how I was to communicate with her without a mirror. Suddenly, it occurred to me that I could try using the magic of technology. I swiped the screen to my phone and touched the camera button, and as if taking a selfie, I turned the lens to reflect my face. I saw my digital reflection on my phone and proceeded to call out Serena's name. And then just as what I experienced in my bathroom mirror, I saw a white mist of smoke fill my phone screen, and within seconds, Serena's face appeared on my phone.

"Serena?" I whispered, realizing my headphones were still plugged in.

"Yes, it is me. I am sorry we could not speak longer the last time, but I sensed someone was coming," said Serena.

"I understand. It was Ms. Pike who interrupted us last time," I added.

"I see. I am sure you have questions, so I am here now to answer as much as you need," said Serena.

"You bet I have questions! Where do I start?" I asked.

"Start with the one thing that is troubling you the most," said Serena.

"Okay," I said, pausing for a few seconds trying to gather a coherent thought. "How do I learn to develop my magic? I asked.

"Well, to begin, you will need to learn to clear your mind. Once you do that, you then need to visualize the energy force that is needed to allow magic to flow," said Serena.

"How do you visualize something you can't touch coming to you?" I asked.

"Emily, magical energy is all around you and in everything that lives and breathes. You will feel it. Once you do, you then need to draw its force inside you. Harness it and then allow it to flow through you. Once you can feel the flow of the energy force, your magic awakens. Once the magic is released, it transforms into whatever you choose it to be," said Serena.

"When I was on the beach with Sam, I could feel an energy flow through me. What was that?" I asked.

"Yes, I drew the force into you, and the energy flow you sensed was you harnessing it. I then helped guide you toward transforming the energy into magic—the magic of healing was the result," said Serena.

"I see, so the glow of my hands was a sign magic is happening?" I asked.

"Yes, your hands will act like your magic wand, in a sense," said Serena.

"I think I am starting to understand," I said with more clarity.

"Good. But know that in the beginning, it is important to practice this act of energy channeling. To help you visual this, close your eyes and try to picture how it feels when sunlight hits your body, feel the warmth. Now, instead of feeling the sun's sensation, imagine the energy force you are trying to draw in. Remember, anything that lives or breathes is or has an energy force. The more you get used to drawing in these forces naturally, the quicker your magic will come to you. Once you learn to control the magic as it flows through you, you will be able to mold it, shape it, and maybe even change it. I cannot begin to explain how much power you have, Emily. It will come when you are ready," said Serena.

"What about the chanting and the words I heard on the beach? Will I have to know them?" I asked.

"In order to awaken you, I had to use a spell from the book of the Mystics, since it was the book that also allowed me to transfer my magic to you back in the cavern. For centuries, I used chants alongside my magic, but that was my time. Your magic is different, as is your time will be different," Serena added.

"Do you think we can try something? I mean, magic?" I asked, curious to feel the energy flow I felt on the beach again.

"Yes, let's try something," Serena said in agreement.

As I prepared to practice my new skill, I worried that Sam would awaken. When I looked over at him, I saw he was still sleeping and heavily snoring. I was pretty sure nothing was going to wake him at this point.

"Okay, we can try something simple and not too loud," I said.

Serena nodded.

I closed my eyes and cleared my mind like Serena instructed.

"Now stick your hand out the window," said Serena.

I lifted my right hand out the window and felt the cool breeze brush against my palm. In my mind, I pictured the sunlight beating down on my arm and hand. Then as Serena said, I changed the image of the sun to wind. I held the thought for a few minutes until I started to feel the chill of the wind slowly creep up my arm and then into my body. I felt as though I had just jumped into ice-cold bath. I was engulfed by the feeling of pins and needles throughout my entire body. But strangely, I felt no pain. Placed in front of me was a stainless steel water canister I was going to take with me on the hike.

"Hold the canister with your other hand, Emily," said Serena.

I placed my left hand around the canister.

"What you have harnessed, now allow magic to happen and transform," said Serena.

I watched as my hand started to glow, this time light blue in color. The feeling of icicles left my body and travelled to another place. In my mind, the thought of icicles caused the light blue glow in my hands to sustain for a few seconds, and then it slowly subsided. When I removed my hand from the canister, I saw the canister had changed, as did its contents inside. A layer of frost painted the entire outside of my canister, and when I lifted it, the water inside was completely frozen.

"Well done, Emily," said Serena, noticing my accomplishment.

"That was amazing," I said.

I looked down at my hands and began to understand the power they possessed. I was beginning to understand Serena's magic too. Now, I just needed to figure out how to make it my own. I truly believed that would be a lesson for another time.

"Emily," Serena called out. "Remember, this is just the beginning. Where you go from here will be determined by you. There will always be challenges especially when dark magic is encountered," Serena added.

"Dark magic?" I asked.

"Yes. Dark magic uses and draws on the same energy forces you do. However, the result is usually to cause harm or evil," said Serena.

"Who would use dark magic?" I asked.

"Those consumed by hatred and soul-less hearts will be drawn to the evil side of magic and will use it for their own selfish gain," said Serena.

I knew the evil Serena described. I had faced that before with Gideon. Yet with Gideon, the threat was his supernatural strength and abilities. The thought of having to face someone just as evil, this time with magical powers, would be just as dangerous or perhaps even more. I feared I would not be ready for that challenge.

"So, magic is determined by the conjurer?" I asked.

"Correct. It is a person's essence that will determine whether they will travel down an evil path or a good path," said Serena

"What's to stop me from using dark magic or travelling down the wrong path?" I asked.

"Emily, I chose you because I already sensed the purity and goodness in you. I knew my magic would continue to help those in need because at the heart of who you are is someone who will always want to protect and help all who need it," said Serena.

I nodded and looked over at Sam. What Serena had said was true, and Sam was proof.

"Emily, I will need to warn you about your friend," said Serena.

"You mean Sam?" I asked.

"Yes," said Serena.

"What about Sam?" I questioned, curious about Serena's comment.

"Sam will face a battle within himself. He will feel lost and unsure. Your friendship will be his light during his darkness, and your power can help change him," said Serena.

"Me? What can I do?" I asked.

"You will know when the time comes, I promise," said Serena, as her image slowly began to fade out.

I watched as Serena's face disappeared and my face appeared on my phone's screen. I could not help but wonder what Serena meant about Sam. Until I remembered Sam did have something to tell me. I wondered if there was a connection between what Sam had to tell me and what Serena warned me about. I needed to know. Out of pure curiosity, I moved toward Sam's side of the back seat and attempted to awaken him. Sam's groggy head wobbled back and forth as I shook his arm. I continued my attempt. Just when I had him almost awake, I heard my father's voice call out from the driver's side.

"Get ready you two. We will be at the ranger's station in two minutes," he hollered.

Sam's eyes finally opened once he heard my father's voice. Sam rubbed his eyes and stretched his arms over his head.

"Thanks, Emily, for waking me up just in time," said Sam, continuing to stretch.

"I actually woke you up for another reason, but I guess that will have to wait now," I said, slightly disappointed.

Sam looked at me, trying to figure out what I meant, and then remembered. "You wanted to know what I had to say?" said Sam, realizing the reason for my dismay.

I nodded.

"Let me ask you this first, who were you talking to on your phone?" asked Sam.

"You were awake?" I asked curiously.

"Kind of, I was in and out, but I did open my eyes and saw you talking to your screen with your headphones plugged in. I wasn't paying too much attention to what you were saying. I was more interested in going back to sleep," said Sam.

"I was talking to Serena," I said.

"Really? She makes phone calls now?" said Sam with a chuckle.

"No. I used the camera on my phone to get my digital reflection," I said.

"That's brilliant," said Sam, clapping his hands in praise.

Just as I was about to go into more details about what Serena and I spoke about, the Jeep came to a halt. We had arrived at the ranger's station. I sighed, hoping to have the chance to continue our conversation; but unfortunately, it was going to have to wait. Now both Sam and I had a secret to share yet needed to find the right moment. Little did we know, it was going to be a moment that we both had not planned on, and the timing of that moment would be determined by the moon.

Chapter

9

The ranger's station was a wooden dark-green cabin situated in the heart of the forest. In front of the cabin was a small parking lot paved by gravel stones. The gravel stones had not been filled for some time, so in several gravel gaps, small patches of grass protruded through. This was where the Jeep pulled into. As everyone stepped out of the Jeep, the view of the cabin was encompassed by forest and shrubbery. Taking a quick glance at the wall of trees, one could see a few dirt paths that started from the cabin and led into the woods. Sam's curiosity got the best of him. I watched Sam wander toward each of the paths, running into each entrance and then out again of each. When Sam called out for me to join him, I could not refuse the adventurous invitation, so I followed.

The front door to the cabin swung open, and out walked a tall, bearded, brown-haired gentleman wearing a Parks and Recreation uniform. The gentleman moved directly toward Daniel.

"Daniel!" called the man.

Daniel extended his hand out to the gentleman. "Rick, how are you?"

"Well, I could be better. But it is good to see you," said Rick.

"Thanks again for meeting us and giving us a hand," said Daniel.

"I think I should be one thanking you. If there is a dangerous animal in my forest, then no one should be getting hurt. So, you say you have someone who encountered it?" asked Rick.

"Yes, and he is here with us," said Daniel.

Daniel called out for Sam and Emily, but it was only Cy that met up behind him holding the gear from the Jeep.

"Did you see Emily and Sam?" asked Daniel to Cy.

"No. They were supposed to help me with the gear, but when I turned around, they were gone," said Cy with a grunt.

"We will have to put a shorter leash on those two. Cy, this is my friend Rick," said Daniel.

"Hello. Nice to meet you. Daniel says you know these woods very well," said Cy.

"Nice to meet you, Cy. And yes, I have been coming here for years, and when I got hired as park ranger, it seemed like a good fit for me," said Rick.

"So, did you let Rick in on our plan?" asked Cy.

"I was just about to," said Daniel.

"I see you have some camping gear?" asked Rick.

"Yes, we figure the hike will take us a few hours, which will be close to nightfall. So instead of heading back tonight, we were going to camp out and head back tomorrow during the day," said Daniel.

"Okay, well, let's head inside and check out the trail maps. I know I will not be able to camp out with you tonight because I have to be back at the station before nightfall," said Rick, opening the door to allow Daniel and Cy to step inside.

All three men stood around Rick's desk as he laid out a large map. Rick proceeded to indicate the areas Daniel and Cy were to check out.

"I can only accompany you to Hawk Eye's ridge, which is only a couple hours from here. A couple of the areas I just showed you are on the way. While the other is just past the ridge," said Rick.

"That's fine. I will scan the map with my phone and load it into my computer. Then I can input the coordinates of each area into the GPS on my watch," said Cy as he raised his phone to the map.

"Got to love technology these days," said Rick with a laugh.

"Well, with Cy, we expect nothing less," said Daniel.

"Sounds like I won't have to worry about you guys getting lost out there," said Rick.

"Copy that," said Cy.

"My only concern is if you end up finding what you are looking for. What kind of animal are you looking for, by the way? " asked Rick.

"The animal we are looking for is quite large and of the canine species," added Cy.

"Canine?" questioned Rick

"Yes, it's a—" Just as Daniel was about to answer Rick, Sam and Emily stormed the cabin door laughing and out of breath.

"Wolf," said Daniel, finishing his thought and, with a look of annoyance, turned toward the two teenagers.

"Sorry, Father, we were checking out the trails at the back," I said.

"I'm sorry too, Daniel. It's my fault. I couldn't help myself. I have always loved being in and around woods, I dragged Emily along," said Sam, trying to appear apologetic.

Daniel just shook his head.

"Rick, this is my daughter, Emily, and this is Sam," said Daniel.

Rick glanced toward Emily's direction and nodded. Then Rick turned toward Sam and walked closer, as if sensing something familiar. Sam stood still while Rick circled around him. Sam wasn't sure what to make of Rick's peculiar actions. So instead, he extended his hand out for a greeting.

"Nice to meet you," said Sam.

Rick shook Sam's hand and continued to stare at him. "Have we met before?" asked Rick.

"No, we have not. I'm new to this area. Just practically got into town," said Sam.

"Rick, Sam is the one who witnessed the wolf attack," said Daniel.

"Interesting. So, you saw the animal up close?" asked Rick with an inquisitive look.

"Yes, sir," said Sam, suddenly feeling Rick's authority over him.

Rick had not let go of Sam's hand. Rick then pulled Sam closer to him. "Did the wolf attack you?" asked Rick.

"It tried. But I managed to escape," said Sam, trying to maneuver out from Rick's grip.

Rick noticed Sam's subtle struggle and finally released his grip from Sam's hand and stepped away from the boy.

"And you all plan on camping out there tonight?" asked Rick.

"Well, that is the plan," said Daniel.

"Okay then, let me just change my clothes and grab my gear. I will be out in just a few minutes if you want to wait out by your Jeep," said Rick heading toward a back room.

Daniel nodded and led the group through the front door and outside to the Jeep.

Rick listened for Daniel's entourage to exit the cabin. He walked into the back room and closed the door. He leaned against the wall by the door and covered his face with his hands. Rick could feel the guilt of his actions. He knew what Sam was or what was going to be. He debated back and forth in his mind whether he should warn the rest of their danger. He concluded that none of them knew because if they did, camping tonight would not have been an option. As he changed his shirt and pulled out his backpack from the closet, he decided he would find out as much as he could or perhaps try and prevent what he could.

Chapter

10

Rick rejoined the crew waiting by the Jeep. Daniel and Cy strapped on their DES utility belts while Rick clipped his last buckle to his backpack to his waist.

"Everyone all set?" asked Daniel father.

"Check," replied Cy.

"All good here," said Sam and Emily in unison.

"Let's head this way down this trail," said Rick, leading the group toward the back of the cabin down one of the trails Sam and Emily ventured through when they first arrived.

The group travelled through the trees and down a dirt trail that, in the beginning, appeared very narrow for a few meters. Then after the trail widened, no longer did they have to walk single file, one behind the other, but rather, now they could walk two by two. Rick walked beside Daniel while Cy moved to the head, checking the GPS on his watch. At the rear, Sam and Emily travelled together in a pair. After about an hour of hiking the trail, they came to a small stream where Daniel decided to allow the group to rest for a while until they moved forward again.

"The water here is drinkable, if anyone is thinking about filling their water cannisters," said Rick.

"Good timing, my bottle was running low, and I am working up a sweat out here," said Sam, crouching down to refill his water bottle.

"How can you be warm? I'm wearing a thermal long sleeve and a hoody, and I'm still chilly," Emily said.

"You are a girl," said Sam, taking off his sweater and wrapping it around his waist.

Emily giggled and scooped up some water from the stream and splashed in Sam's direction. "Here, that should cool you off."

Rick watched as the two youngsters continued to play by the stream. He figured now would be a good time to intervene.

"Sam!" Rick called. "Can I talk to you for a minute?"

Sam left Emily's side and walked over to Rick, who sat on a rock away from the rest of group.

"What's up?" asked Sam, walking up to Rick.

"You might want to consider coming back with me and not camp out with the rest of the others," said Rick.

"Why would I do that?" questioned Sam.

"Let's just say you might put them in danger tonight. The same danger you experienced the last time you were in these woods," said Rick.

"What are you talking about?" asked Sam, completely baffled.

"Let me ask you this, have you been feeling different lately? Has your body become so warm at times and you are not sure why? Also, while hiking today, does the forest appear different to you now? What do you hear, and what do you smell?" said Rick.

Sam paused and looked at Rick, as if he knew everything that was happening inside him. *Impossible*, Sam thought.

"Believe it or not, we are the same, Sam. You and I share a secret that no one here knows about," said Rick, creeping closer to Sam to avoid being overheard by the others.

"I don't know what is happening to me," said Sam, growing agitated.

"I can tell it is just the beginning for you. If you have not completed the transformation, then you will tonight. That is why I want you to come back with me," said Rick with a serious tone.

"The beginning of what transformation? " demanded Sam.

Rick could see Sam was not grasping the seriousness of his warning.

"There is a folklore that my great-grandfather used to tell me about. It was about a wolf. This wolf was unlike any normal wolf. Not only was its size bigger than any normal wolf, but it also had a curse, which some say originated from a witch. The animal was cursed with being a human during the day and an animal at night. At night, the animal is purely instinctive. It hunts, and it kills. My great-grandfather told me that if anyone is ever bitten by this wolf and not killed, they too will become the same. And the curse continues to another. It is the curse of the wolfman, and it's not just a story. It's true," said Rick, leaning back and folding his arms.

Sam listened to Rick. And then began to recall his attack, the scar it left behind, and what he felt last night in his room. As the flood of thoughts filled his mind, he slowly started to realize what Rick was warning him about.

"Are you saying I am cursed?" asked Sam.

"Yes, you are," said Rick.

"Then that means you are too?" said Sam.

"Yes, I am. And if I were you, don't tell anyone about our secret. They couldn't understand or won't even believe you. Trust me," said Rick sternly.

Sam knew he had a choice to make. But was he not ready to make it at that moment. He needed more time to decide and be sure. He had just met Rick and debated on how much he could trust him or not. Sam also now understood Rick's odd attention toward him at the cabin.

"I need more time to think things through," said Sam.

"Well, you have until we reach Hawk Eye's Ridge. Then you will have to make a choice," said Rick.

Sam nodded and headed back to the others.

—◊—

My father leaned against a tree trunk, debating on the next course of action for the group. "How far until Hawk Eye's Ridge?" my father asked Cy.

"According to my GPS, we should reach it in just under an hour," added Cy.

"Rick, are we close to one of the areas you mentioned back at the cabin?" my father asked.

"Yes, this is it, as a matter of fact," hollered Rick from his perch.

"Makes sense, the stream would act as water source for the animal," said Cy.

"Everyone, spread out and take a look around but stay close to the stream," said Daniel.

Everyone did as my father instructed, each moving in different directions. Rick was the only one who stayed rooted at his spot. After several minutes, the group gathered back with no proof of any tracks or evidence of the animal. My father decided it was best to keep moving toward Hawk Eye's Ridge. As everyone gathered their belongings to begin the trek, I noticed how quiet Sam had been since his conversation with Rick.

"So, what did Rick have to say to you?" I asked.

"Oh, he kept asking about my attack," said Sam, sounding evasive.

"Are you sure that was it? He was acting very odd with you back at the cabin, I thought maybe it had to do with that?" I persisted.

"It was nothing! So just drop it, okay?" said Sam as he walked away.

—m—

As Sam walked ahead of Emily, he felt the guilt of not being truthful. He wanted to tell Emily everything, but also wanted to not worry her. Sam still believed there was a chance Rick could be wrong. In the back of Sam's mind, he also wondered what if Rick was right and he was going to change tonight. Did he want to put everyone he has grown to care about in danger? *I am not a killer,* he thought. Sam remembered how he fought the urges last night and he wondered if he would be able to do it again, or would the transformation be more intense and uncontrollable this time.

"We are coming up to the coordinates of the other possible sighting area," shouted Cy to the group.

As the group halted in a small clearing, they again were instructed by Daniel to fan out and search for clues of the animal. Rick was the only one who stuck closer to Sam while everyone went off in different directions. Sam tried to avoid another confrontation with Rick, but Rick's persistence was evitable.

"Ticktock, boy," hollered Rick as he caught up to Sam on the trail.

Sam glared at Rick.

"So where is your head at, boy?" probed Rick.

"Why can't I tell my friends about all of this? We are out here trying to find the one thing you won't let me to tell them about. It's not fair," said Sam.

"Trust me, let them be. You know they are not going to find anything unless you stay with them. I have spent months trying to contain myself to prevent any accidents. I haven't wanted to hurt anyone either, but it is the animal inside that makes me do it. Every day, I wish I did not have this, but somehow, it was given to me. Now, because of my mistake, so do you," said Rick.

"Your mistake?" questioned Sam.

"Yes, one night, I was drunk and careless and did not cage myself. That was the same night we first met. The campfire, the broken wooden box, and the fangs—that was me. I chased you into the woods toward the river and left you with a bite before I fell off the cliff into the rapids," confessed Rick.

"That was you? How do you remember all that if you were an animal?" asked Sam.

"As an animal, it is still my eyes they are seeing through. The instincts are primal, but my human self is still there behind the eyes," said Rick, pointing to his face.

Sam stopped walking and leaned against a tree trunk as panic started to swell within him. The animal he thought he killed was not dead. It stood before him, and now, the truth about what he was to become was also coming to light. Sam's panic grew, and he lashed out at Rick.

"You did this to me! It is your fault! What kind of life am I to live now?" yelled Sam. In anger, he pushed Rick away.

Rick continued to take on Sam's rage, "I can teach you!" Rick replied.

Sam's rage continued. He lashed out and shoved Rick one last time. The shove accidentally forced Rick backward where a fallen tree trunk stood at Rick's feet. The bearded man fell backward while tripping over the trunk. Sam watched as Rick's fall ended in tragedy. For it was not the soft blades of grass that broke Rick's fall; instead, it was a large hidden rock embedded in the shrubbery that was to blame for the injury to the back of Rick's head. The accident left Rick's body unconscious and lying on the grass. Sam's rage turned into fear as he instantly screamed for help.

Sam hoped that his cry was heard by someone from his group. Rick lay motionless on the ground. Sam began to panic. He didn't want to cause any harm; he was upset and lashed out in anger. *It was an accident*, he thought. As Sam reached his hand under Rick's head to cradle it away from the rock, he noticed a small amount of blood coming from the base of Rick's head. Sam immediately grabbed his sweater to apply pressure to the wound. Just then, he heard Rick groan. Sam called out to Rick to awaken him. Unfortunately, Rick was not able to stay conscious. Sam called out for help once again. Daniel and Cy were the first to arrive.

"What happened?" asked Daniel, laying his backpack to the ground beside Rick.

"He tripped on the tree branch, fell back, and hit his head on this rock," said Sam, pointing to the culprit next to them.

"Daniel, the base of his head is injured. We need to try and get him conscious," said Cy.

Daniel called out to Rick while Cy assessed Rick's legs. Cy was able to deduce that nothing appeared broken, but without Rick being able to wake up, there was no way to know if he was in any pain. Just then, Rick let out another groan; and this time, his eyes slowly began to open.

"Rick! Can you hear me?" asked Daniel.

"Daniel," Rick moaned.

"Yes, tell me where you hurt?" asked Daniel once again.

"My ankle and my head," mumbled Rick.

Cy pulled out the medical bag from his backpack and shuffled through it.

"How's the blood flow from his head?" asked Cy.

"Looks like the bleeding has slowed down a bit. Good work, Sam," said Daniel, turning to Sam.

Sam smiled as he continued to hold the sweater to Rick's head.

"We need to move him to a more open area to treat his wounds," said Cy.

Daniel, Sam, and Cy slowly lifted Rick away from the tree branch and placed him on a flat grassier surface. Rick drifted in and out while the men worked to assess what needed to be done. Daniel looked down at his watch.

"We lost a lot of daylight during our search at both areas. We can either head back now or camp here for the night," said Daniel.

"If we head back now, we can use my disks to transport Rick so there would be no need to carry him. And that should save us some travelling time," said Cy.

"That's a good idea. However, my only concern is that we will be walking back in the dark during nightfall," said Daniel.

"I think it is risk we will need to take. My concern is Rick's head injury. Without proper medical care, it could lead to more serious complications," said Cy.

"I agree. Rick needs medical attention, and that should be our priority. Prepare your disks," said Daniel.

"Copy that. First, I will need to inject Rick with some pain medication and bandage up his head before we are set to travel," added Cy.

"Good. I'll try and track down Emily so we can all leave together," said Daniel.

"Sam, I will need you to help me with Rick," said Cy.

"Sure. What do you need, Cy?" asked Sam.

Sam hunched over Cy's backpack, pulling out bandages, while Cy prepared the syringe with the pain medication. Daniel stood up from the ground and looked around. *Where is Emily?* he wondered.

Chapter

11

The area I wandered into was full of low-lying bushes all staggered and spread throughout a vast meadow. The open space was warm and filled with wildflowers of many different colors. For a few minutes, I was lost in the picturesque scenery, and I hadn't even realized how far I wandered from our meeting point. While walking through the tall grass and wildflowers, I had the sudden urge to practice magic. I found a spot in the middle of the meadow surrounded by randomly scattered boulders. I noticed the boulders varied in size, yet most were too big to lift on my own while some appeared embedded in the ground. I stretched out my arms, knelt to the ground, and placed my palms unto the grassy plain. I closed my eyes and slowed down my breathing to enter a more meditative state. Within seconds, a surge of energy began to flow through me, and I began to sense the firmness of the ground travel through my fingertips and up to my entire body. In my mind, I saw an ocean of feathers floating. Suddenly, I began to feel the ground begin to rumble. When I opened my eyes, I saw small dirt pebbles from ground tremble beneath me. Then my hands began glowing, this time green in color. The rumbling grew louder. As my hands continued to glow, I saw one of the large boulders shake as if trying to free itself from the ground. Then I saw another do the same while other boulders not embedded in the ground began to simply float and rise above the grass and flowers. I had learned to levitate objects. I rose from my kneeling position with my arms still stretched out. The glow from my hands had not subsided as it did before. I was able to hold the glow at will. I also discovered that I could control the boulders' movements. I could make them all rise higher or push them forward and pull them back. I was able to hold my right arm in place and wave the left arm to control individual boulders, as a conductor would do in front of an orchestra. I was connected to the boulders, and they were connected to me. I could feel the energy flow through and surround me, especially in this open area of the meadow. It was a feeling more powerful than the cannister in the Jeep. I wondered if I could stretch out to connect with other energy forces while I was still connected to the boulders. I could sense the other energies, and I wanted to attempt to tap into them as well. I wanted to try.

Just as I was about to make my attempt, a sudden cry echoed from the woods and caught my attention. The distraction was so intense the boulders abruptly fell to the ground with a resounding thud, ending our magical connection. And just as one connection ended, another was made. I was overcome by the feeling of fear, and then a vision of Sam flashed in my mind. I ran into the woods.

I ran aimlessly through the trees and dirt paths, hoping to find my way. But I was lost. I only heard the cry once and really needed to hear it again to know what direction I needed to take. So, I called out Sam's name, but I heard nothing back. I needed help to find Sam. Just then where I stood, I noticed a saw a small pool of water. I bent down to my knees and looked at the water's surface, hoping to find my reflection. To my relief, there I was, and then I knew what I needed to do next. I called out Serena's name. The surface of the water and my reflection changed into the face of Serena.

"Emily, what is wrong?" asked Serena.

"I'm in the woods trying to find my way to Sam. I heard him call out, and I could sense he is in trouble. What do I do?" I pleaded.

"Emily, the fact you can sense him is the key to finding him. Take a small thin branch with a pointy tip and place it on the water surface," said Serena.

I did as Serena said and found a small thin twig with a pointy edge to place on the water and watched it float, "Now what?"

"Now, clear your mind and think only of Sam," said Serena.

Again, I did as Serena said. I closed my eyes and focused all my thoughts on Sam.

"Good, Emily. Now, place your hand over the water," added Serena.

As I placed my hand over the water, I could feel my palm pulse. It was a feeling as if I had my hand place over someone's heart, and I could feel their heartbeat. Just as the pulsing continued, I noticed the twig begin to circle, just as a needle inside a compass would. The twig continued circling as I continued to focus on Sam. Just then, a flash of Sam's face appeared in my mind, and at the same time, the twig stopped circling. The pointy edge of the twig gave me the direction I needed to take. I thanked Serena and dashed off into Sam's direction once again.

Chapter

12

Daniel watched as Sam finished wrapping the last bandage around Rick's head while Cy pulled out the disks from his belt to engage the transportation device. Sam stepped back from Rick's body as Cy's disks moved through the air, stopped, and then hovered over Rick's body. With a few taps on his cell phone, Cy programmed the disks to initiate the invisible barrier around Rick's body. The barrier was not completely transparent, Cy added a white shade so one could see the boxlike shape of the barrier. Once the barrier was set, Cy set another command with his cell phone to transport. Within seconds, Rick's entire body began to levitate a few feet off the ground, and the boxlike cloud that held Rick started to move forward. Sam's eyes widened.

"How are you doing this, Cy?" asked Sam in amazement.

"Nano-bots, my boy, they are called nano-bots," said Cy, inputting the final command on his phone before sliding it back into his pocket.

"Are we ready?" asked Daniel to Cy.

Cy walked over to the barrier to give it his final inspection and then replied, "Yes, we are good to go. The barrier is now programmed to follow behind us, and it will move when we move," said Cy.

"Great, now all we need is my daughter before we completely lose what daylight we have," said Daniel.

Daniel's fatherly instincts rose to the surface *Where is she?* he wondered as he drew his attention toward the darkening forest that surrounded them.

Oddly, Sam's attention was also drawn to the forest. The more he focused on the forest, the more he suddenly could hear the sounds coming from within the woods. The slight rustle of the trees appeared louder to him, and even the small movements made by the squirrels and chipmunks were clearly distinctive to his ears. The more intently he listened, the more he could hear the forest speak through movement. As strange as it felt to him at that moment, it also felt very natural, almost instinctive. Sam walked closer to the tree line and scanned it, as if trying to get a sense of Emily's whereabouts. As he drew closer to the edge of the tree line, he walked along the outer edge of the trees, trying to focus on what was behind the trees. Sam then abruptly stopped.

"Sam what are you doing," Cy called out from a few feet away.

Distracted by what he was hearing and now smelling, he didn't realize how far he had distanced himself from Daniel and Cy. The two men watched as Sam ran toward a certain tree line of the forest.

"I think he is tracking," said Cy.

"That does not look like tracking to me. It looks more like an animal sensing their prey," said Daniel.

Sam was certain he caught a whiff of Emily's scent coming from a certain tree line and scrub grouping. It was the smell of Emily's hair that caused him to dart into the woods and disappear from Cy's and Daniel's sight.

"Where did he go? He was just there!" said Cy, pointing off to an area ahead of them.

"We need to seriously put a leash on that boy. Looks like he went into the woods," said Daniel, motioning Cy to move toward the area Sam was last seen.

As Daniel and Cy moved down the tree line, Rick's lifeless body in the barrier followed behind them. With each step they took, the barrier did as it was supposed to, like a trained horse.

Sam, now inside the walls of the trees, tried to track what direction Emily's scent was coming from. When he turned his head to the right, there it was. The scent was stronger in that direction. Sam started to pick up his pace, and as he did, he could hear tiny tree branches breaking. He knew he was heading in the right direction.

"Emily!" Sam called out.

And, there it was. Sam's call was the sound I needed to hear to know for sure I was heading in the right direction. I quickened my pace and called back out to him, hoping he would hear it. Sam, this time, heard my call back.

"Emily, I'm coming," Sam called.

"Sam, I hear you," I said.

Sam continued to move quickly through the forest, dodging fallen tree branches and leaping over fallen tree trunks, trying to get to Emily. Sam would not let go of Emily's scent and followed it persistently without paying any attention to the pitfalls that may lie ahead. Pitfalls only a forest could hold especially when others who venture into it look to trap unwilling prey. Sam mistakenly leaped over a fallen trunk and found himself plunging through a pile of scrubs and branches. The camouflage was used to conceal a deep hole. The hole was meant for trapping a large animal; however, it trapped Sam instead.

Not hearing Sam's voice for a short time, I called out, "Sam, are you still out there?" I slowed my pace down as I tried to hear Sam's reply.

"Sam!" I called out again.

No answer from Sam. I grew concerned.

At the bottom of the hole, Sam regained his senses to view his dirty surroundings. He also felt a sharp pain coming from his ankle. The fall was quite long, and he must have tweaked it when he landed, he thought. With the injured foot and the depth of the hole, Sam knew climbing out was not an option. Sam also knew Emily was still out there and tried to call back out to her.

—⟪⟫—

I was relieved to finally hear Sam's cry, but the sound of his cry was unlike the previous one.

"Sam, are you alright?" I shouted.

"Emily, I fell into what looks like a giant pit," shouted Sam. I rushed to find Sam.

Sam continued to call out to me, hoping his voice would draw me closer. I finally managed to find the hole Sam was trapped in.

"Sam, I'm here," I yelled, lying on my belly, peering down into the dark pit.

"Emily, I'm down here," replied Sam, trying to move into what little light there was so I could see him.

"Are you hurt?" I asked.

"I think I tweaked my ankle a bit. I am having a hard time standing on it," Sam said.

"What were you doing out here anyway?" I asked.

"I was trying to find you," said Sam.

I laughed. "Some rescue! Looks, like I'm going to have to bail you out again."

"Just so you know, I am not keeping score!" hollered Sam.

I laughed again, "I heard you calling for help, so I was trying to find you. Where's my father and Cy?" I finally asked.

"I left them at the edge of the tree line. Rick got hurt. They are with him." said Sam.

"What happened to Rick?" I asked curiously.

"Rick and I got into it, and I shoved him. His ankle got messed up, and he hit head on a rock. We were about to head back as soon as we found you. Emily, it's all my fault," said Sam.

"What do you mean?" I asked.

"It's my fault Rick got hurt. I lost my temper," said Sam.

"Sam, Rick must have said something for that to happen. You are not the type who would hurt anyone intentionally," I said. "What did Rick say?" I then asked.

"Rick said that I would be putting you all in danger. He said there is something about me that I can't tell you about because you wouldn't believe me or understand. And that only he can help me with," said Sam.

"Do you believe him?" I asked.

"At first I didn't. But then I started to see that what he was saying could be true. Emily, what if I am putting you all in danger? I don't think I could forgive myself if I hurt you or any of your family," said Sam with a frustrated sigh. "You know what, maybe it is best if you just leave me here. Get your family and yourself as far away from me as possible," said Sam as he leaned his head against the dirt wall of the hole.

I laughed again at Sam's semi melt-down. "Well, that's not going to happen anytime soon, trust me. We are going to find a way to get you out of here, and whatever Rick told you, we will deal with together, no matter what it is. Sam, I know you would not let anything bad happen to me because I know I would do the same for you. Believe in that. So, stay put while I get my father and Cy. I think one of them packed some rope," I said.

"Yes, ma'am. If you head west toward the tree line, you will find them," said Sam.

—◊◊◊—

Left alone in the hole, Sam's thoughts drifted to thinking, "*once I transform, if I transform nothing would be the same again. And, as the day grows darker and darker it would be just a matter of hours before we all find out,*"

—◊◊◊—

I reached the edge of the tree line like Sam mentioned and saw my father and Cy, with a floating Rick behind them.

"Father!" I cried out.

"Emily! Did Sam find you?" yelled my father while running toward me.

"Yes! Sam is stuck in a hole. He fell into one while he was trying to find me. We need to get him out," I said.

While overhearing my plight, Cy ruffled through his backpack and pulled out some rope, a series of clamps, glow sticks, and a couple flashlights he packed. "I have what we need to get Sam out," said Cy.

"Wait, even if we get Sam out of the hole, he will have a hard time walking. He said he hurt his ankle in the fall," I added.

My father looked even more concerned. We had lost the day, and night was upon us. By the time we reached Sam and rescued him from the hole, the trek back to the ranger station he had planned would be completely in darkness. And the light source we brought was not enough for an overnight trek through the woods. My father had no choice but to go with plan C: rescue Sam then camp for the night. At daylight, we could radio the ranger station with Rick's walkie for help and arrange for a pickup, especially now that they would have two injured bodies. My father relayed the plan to Cy and me then asked me to lead them to Sam. My father, Cy, and I along with a floating Rick, some glow sticks, and a couple flashlights, entered the darkening woods to find Sam.

After several minutes, we reached Sam's hole. The hole was pitch-black inside. We called out to Sam to ensure he was still safe. When Sam called out, Cy dropped a couple glow sticks down the hole to give Sam some light.

"Ah, that's much better!" said Sam, appreciating his new light source.

"How's your ankle?" I asked.

"It's definitely swollen," replied Sam.

"Don't worry, once we get you out of here, there's an ice pack here with your name on it," said Cy, unravelling the rope.

Cy looked around to see what he could use to anchor the rope with. Nearby, he noticed a large trunk, so began to fasten the rope there.

"Hey, Sam! So, change of plans. Just so you know, we are not going to hike back to the ranger station tonight. Instead, we will be camping for the night," hollered my father.

"Camping, huh?" said Sam.

"Yeah. I thought you loved camping?" my father said, trying to stall, giving Cy time to finish preparing the line into the hole.

"Well, I guess with my ankle messed up, I wouldn't be in any shape to travel," said Sam.

While my father and Cy worked to prepare the line to pull Sam out, I built a small fire and pulled out the camping gear just a few feet from the hole.

"How's Rick?" asked Sam from the hole.

I caught my father's glance over at Rick's floating body, which hovered slightly by my fire. "Rick's still unconscious. No change really," replied my father to Sam.

Sam knew it was now nightfall, and with no change happening to Rick, it gave him a sense of relief. *Maybe Rick was wrong? Maybe he was just messing with my head?* Sam thought to himself.

"We are just about ready to throw down the rope. Let us know when it reaches you," said Cy.

"Okay, will do," replied Sam.

"Okay here it comes," hollered Cy.

The moon had risen to its place in the night sky. I watched as Cy and my father began Sam's rescue from the hole. I stood by the fire, working to keep it ablaze. I was enjoying the sound of a crackling fire, the warmth of the flames, and the calmness of the night. Suddenly, an odd sound caught my attention. It was faint but sounded like was a low growl then a cracking of sticks. The fire crackled again as I listened intently to more odd sounds now coming from behind me. The sounds were growing louder. I turned around to see what was causing the noise. What I saw left me mesmerizingly paralyzed. And in the pit of my stomach, fear suddenly consumed me. Rick's body was no longer motionless and still. It was moving and convulsing within the barrier. I watched as his fingers started to grow into long claws and his face also began to elongate, making way to a protruding snout. Rick's spine made a cracking sound as he struggled in the barrier to rip off his shirt. With his shirt off, I could clearly see his spine breaking out of his skin and molding into something else. Within seconds, I saw the hair or fur begin to rise out of his arms, his legs, and his body. I could not take my eyes off the transformation. I was frozen. When it was all done, I could see that Rick was no longer a man; he was an animal standing on all fours, staring right at me. It was then I also realized, this was the animal we came to find. I finally found my voice and screamed.

My scream caught my father's attention instantly. While at the same time, Cy's cell phone began to beep and vibrate, as if giving off an alert.

Rick's wolf form was in full transformation and fiercely trying to break out of the barrier, causing Cy's program to go into alert mode. The animal continuously rammed the sides and growled in anger, trying to free itself.

"Emily! Get away from there!" yelled my father, fearing for my safety.

—⁓—

Cy quickly anchored the line and left Sam inside the hole.

"My barrier was not designed to withstand that much force from the inside. It was only meant to transport the animal in a sedated state," yelled Cy, trying desperately to reprogram his phone.

The animal gave another brawling thrash into the invisible walls. The walls faded; the disks released and fell to the ground. The wolf was now free and towering before us in the fire's light. Daniel ran toward Emily and pushed her out of the wolf's path just as the animal was about to the pounce on her. Emily rolled onto the ground and fled into the trees.

"Cy! Grab the utility belts," yelled Daniel.

Cy quickly searched for the DES equipment as the animal continued his rampage through the campsite. Cy managed to find one of the belts and pulled out the tranquilizer bullets. Daniel used pieces of a destroyed tent to fend off the animal. Unfortunately, he also found himself in the animal's growling path, now setting its sights on human prey. Daniel could see the animal clearly now. Its paws were two times the size of his feet while his fangs were sharp and drooling in saliva. The wolf was as massive as Sam described. If the animal pounced on him, there was be no chance to escape. He would be forced to take the weight of the animal and hope to keep its mouth from shredding him to pieces. And just as the animal moved to pounce, Daniel braced for the impact. Yet the impact never came. The animal suddenly veered and yelped in pain. One of Cy's tranquilizer bullet hit the animal in the back. The pain stunned the animal, but not for very long. It regained its stance on all fours and turned to face Cy, looking revengeful. Cy launched another bullet at the animal's head. The animal pulled back its head to brace the impact but still came back for more. Two bullets were not enough to quiet the massive beast. Cy knew he had only found one of the belts. Cy only had one bullet left.

"Daniel, we need the other belt?" shouted Cy.

Daniel searched the wreckage of tents and packs scattered about the camp.

"I'm working on it," replied Daniel.

The animal began to thunder toward Cy once again. Having no option Cy, launched another bullet at the animal's chest just before diving away from its charging path. The animal jerked back from the hit and tumbled onto its back. With three bullets inside it, the beast was only slightly feeling the effects of the tranquilizer. Daniel knew Cy's last hit on the wolf also meant that was Cy's last bullet. Daniel quickly lifted a few pieces of debris, and luckily, the second belt was found. Hoping to draw the animal's attention away from Cy, Daniel called to the wolf. The animal once again regained its stance and began its charge now at Daniel. Daniel watched as the animal raced toward him. Holding all three bullets in his hand, Daniel waited for the right moment. Cy, from a distance, watched the wolf charge and yelled for Daniel to launch the bullets. However, Daniel continued to wait. He knew that the animal was more vulnerable in the chest area based on Cy's last hit. He needed the animal to expose his chest to him, but for that to happen, he would have to wait until the animal leaped into the air and was on top of him. Daniel watched intently the animal's paws. Once he saw the paws lift above the ground, he knew it would be the time to launch. Within seconds, what Daniel waited for came to pass, and the animal lifted into the air. Daniel launched all three bullets and hit the targeted area. The animal jolted back and yelped, this time, very loudly in pain. The animal once again found its footing but, instead of coming in for another attack, bolted into the woods away from the camp and the two men.

"That animal took six bullets," said Cy in astonishment.

"Let's hope that was enough to keep it away for the night," said Daniel.

"I don't think we can handle another attack," added Cy.

"Where's Emily?" asked Daniel.

"I'm here," she said, emerging from the trees.

"Are you okay?" asked Daniel.

"Yes, I'm fine, just a bit shaken. I have never encountered something like that before. Rick transformed into a wolf!" I gasped.

"That was no ordinary wolf, or my tranquilizer bullets would have served its purpose sooner," added Cy.

"Agreed. The transformation itself was something I have only heard about. When I was cursed as a vampire, I had heard stories of another curse placed on by a witch. It caused a man to turn into an animal at night and human by day. And whoever is bitten by this wolf in turn becomes the same—cursed too," said Daniel.

"So, if Rick is the wolf Sam was talking about then...," said Cy.

"And if Sam was bitten...," said Daniel.

—m—

My heart sunk into my stomach as I recalled what Sam told me in the hole and about Rick. *No!* I thought.

Just then, my father, Cy, and I heard a growl coming from beneath the hole Sam was in. In the battle with wolf Rick, we forgot about Sam.

The growling continued followed by heavy animal breathing as the we stood at a distance from the hole. I had to know and see for myself if it was Sam. I broke from my father's guard and scurried to the hole, calling out Sam's name.

"Emily! Don't!" yelled my father.

I refused to listen to him and moved closer to the hole's opening. I saw the light of the glow sticks coming from the dirt but could not see Sam.

I called out once again. "Sam! It's Emily." I moved closer to the edge of the hole. I was one step from the edge when I heard the animal let out a loud howl. Startled, I slipped and fell on my back. Lying on the ground, my attention was captivated by a massive light-brown furry object jumping out of the hole and soaring over me. When I managed to turn my body around, I saw the animal standing on all fours. The wolf stood between me and my father. The wolf looked at my father and then turned his attention to me. I was now caught in the animal's gaze. Fear should have consumed me; fear should have made me paralyzed like it did with Rick, but fear was not what I was feeling. The longer the animal and I were locked in each other's gaze, the more I could see beyond the beast. I saw Sam's eyes. They were blue and human.

"Emily, I will distract it, so you can run," said my father.

"Father! Wait!" I said, hoping for a longer chance to see beyond the human eyes.

"Emily! Run!" my father said as he grabbed a log from the campfire and waved it at the wolf.

The log caught the wolf's attention. My father was now facing the wolf, hoping to draw it away from my direction. The wolf's pace was slow and somewhat calculating, unlike the violent encounter with wolf Rick. I watched as my father moved slowly as to not agitate the animal. The wolf and my father were now locked into a staring match. Both were just waiting to see who was going to act first.

"Cy, do you have any ideas as to how we are going to sedate this thing?" called out my father, still in a circling pace with the animal.

"Well, we are out of tranquilizers. But I might have one more idea if I can find it," said Cy glancing around the camp.

"Emily, I'm going to circle toward you. When I get to you, I want you behind me," said my father with authority.

I agreed.

My father moved toward me, and as he did, the animal also moved to stay at an opposite distance, still focused on him. As soon as my father reached me, he shoved me behind him and continued his slow pace, but this time moving backwards, creating more distance between the animal and us. The wolf did not follow and just watched as my father and I walked farther and farther away.

Cy was able to rifle through the camp unnoticed and found both utility belts. Digging into the pockets, he found one last barrier disk that appeared damaged and one last DES equipment that still had not been tested.

"Father, Sam is still in there," I said.

"What do you mean?" he asked.

"I mean, I believe inside the wolf there is still the human Sam. I see it in his eyes. That is why he will not hurt us," I pleaded.

I saw the look on my father's face, and I knew he could see the conviction in my words. If I truly believed that Sam was still inside the beast, then there would be no way to harm it without hurting Sam.

"Cy, what do you got?" said Daniel.

"Well, to be honest I'm about 50 percent confident in this plan," said Cy.

"That's way below your normal average of confidence. But unfortunately, that's more than what I have right now," replied my father.

"The bad news is I have nothing to sedate it with. But I do have something that might repel the animal," said Cy, who had made his way next to us.

"You mean scare it off, right? 'Cause we can't hurt it," I said.

"Precisely, I hope," said Cy.

We all agreed with Cy's plan and took refuge behind a couple tree trunks that had fallen onto each other from the impact of the wolf Rick's rampage. The wolf before us stayed calm and continued to pace at a distance.

"What is it doing?" I asked.

"Waiting," said my father.

"Waiting for what?" I asked.

"Waiting for us. Like all animals, they are waiting for their prey. It's their nature. If we run, they will follow, and the hunt begins," added Cy.

"Well, it's now or never, Cy," said my father, motioning for Cy to begin his plan.

Cy nodded and grabbed the device from his pocket. My father looked down at the device.

"The garage door opener?" he asked.

"Somewhat. I used its casing, remember? Let's hope my modifications worked," said Cy.

Cy stood up from our wooden barricade and pointed the device in the wolf's direction. The wolf stopped its pace and turned its attention toward a new target. Cy pressed down on the button on top of the device and waited.

"Cy, just do it already!" hollered my father from the ground.

"I just did," replied Cy.

"I couldn't hear anything," said my father.

"You were not supposed to hear anything. Only the animal heard it. Look!" replied Cy.

We lifted our heads above the trunks and watched as the animal frantically shook its head. The more Cy pressed on the button, the more the animal seemed to be disturbed by it.

"It's working! The device is giving off a high frequency that only canines can hear," said Cy.

"Cy, you basically made a dog whistle," I said.

"Yes, but I changed the frequency to deter the animal, not call them," Cy added.

"Brilliant as usual," added my father.

Cy watched as the animal started to back away from us, still shaking its head as if trying to remove the sound from its ears. Cy decided to move from the barricade and push the animal toward the hole.

"Cy don't move too close to it," yelled my father.

"Its fine. The device is working. I'm moving it away from you both, and hopefully, we can trap it in the hole," said Cy.

However, the more Cy pressed the button, the more the rage beneath the beast came alive. The rage Sam fought to keep at bay was rising to the surface. The human voice beneath all the fur was crying out for Cy to stop because he did not want to hurt them. But by then, it was too late. The wolf's rage broke the repelling sound of the device. It lunged far enough at Cy, swinging its giant paw at the device, knocking it out of Cy's hand, sending it flying into the trees.

"Cy!" yelled Daniel, as he jumped from the barricade.

—ɯ—

I watched as both men stood defenseless before a now-raging animal. The animal growled fiercely, showing every inch of his fangs that would be used to penetrate their skin. I knew what a bite would result in, and with this new sudden change in demeanor, this animal had no intention to wound but rather shred its prey into pieces. This was no longer Sam. They had awakened the primal rage and would have to pay a dear price. It was a price I was not ready for them to pay.

—ɯ—

"I'm sorry, Daniel," said Cy with remorse.

Daniel looked at Cy and assumed the animal would have to choose which prey to pounce on first. He saw the look in his friend's eyes and knew the sacrifice he was going to make.

"Cy, don't!" cried Daniel as Cy pushed Daniel out of the animal's path and called the beast toward him.

On the ground, Daniel watched the wolf charge toward Cy who, in his attempt to run, stumbled to his knees. Daniel could not stand to see his friend come to an end this way.

"No!" cried Daniel.

Just as Daniel was about to witness his friend get mauled to death, a tree trunk flying in midair suddenly caught him by surprise. The trunk flew by Daniel, slightly missing Cy but connected with the animal with such force it sent the wolf flying back several feet from them.

Where did that come from? thought Daniel, completely stunned by what he just saw.

Daniel turned around to see what caused the flying tree. When he turned his head, he found Emily standing by the barricade with glowing green hands.

"Emily?" questioned Daniel, in awe.

"Cy! Father! Run!" she yelled.

Both men watched in amazement and quickly moved out of my path. They continued to watch as I lifted my arms, almost willing the other tree trunk into the air. The wolf regained its balance and was once again ready to charge, this time toward me. But by now, I had the other tree trunk ready and magically launched it toward the animal. The second blow was even more powerful that the animal flew back farther and this time into the hole it originated from. When I approached the hole's edge, I was relieved to see that the animal was still alive. And with a smile, I levitated both trunks back toward me and placed them over the hole. Next, I bent down onto the ground and laid my hands onto the dirt. The green glow continued, and instantly, roots from all nearby trees broke from the dirt and covered the hole, creating a prison. The impenetrable cage was of thick, sturdy tree root that protruded from the dirt and wrapped over the tree trunks, sealing any chance for escape. We were safe. I had bought us enough time for daylight to arrive and for my friend Sam to come back.

Chapter

13

Rick awoke to the sight of daylight rays penetrating through the trees and beaming onto his face. He lifted his hand to his face to shield him from the annoying light. When he regained his clear sense of vision, he looked around at his surroundings. He noticed he was still in the woods and unclothed. It was obvious he had transformed last night, but the awakening this time left him feeling weak and in pain especially at his chest. When Rick peered down at his chest, he could see the wounds that were inflicted from the night. He recalled the bullets that were shot into him. Under normal circumstances, his transformation usually quickened the healing process of any wound he encountered as a human. He felt no pain at the base of his head where he remembered falling after arguing with Sam. Nor did he feel the pain of his ankle when he tripped over the branch. However, during this morning's awakening, the wounds inflicted when he was a wolf were slow to heal. Rick struggled to rise to his feet. After much effort, Rick stood tall and looked around to gain his bearings. He knew where he was, and he knew that he was not far from his home. Naked and in pain, Rick ventured through the forest, finding path after path that would eventually draw him closer to home. With each step he took, Rick began to recall the night's events. He remembered the battle between him and Daniel and Cy. He remembered transforming while in the invisible cage. And most importantly, he remembered that the secret he had kept hidden from everyone all this time was finally exposed. There were now others who knew what he really was, and the fact that he did survive would mean there could be a chance he would have to face them all again.

Rick finally reached his cabin. He pushed open the door and stumbled to the floor. He was weak and dehydrated. He grabbed a throw blanket from his couch and wrapped it around his waist so that some part of him felt clothed. He pulled himself off the floor and walked toward his kitchen table. On the table he saw the indigo-blue bottle and instinctively assumed he had found something to aid in his thirst. He snatched the bottle from the table. He was relieved to feel some weight to the bottle, which meant something was inside. He brought the cork to his teeth and pulled it free. As Rick shook the bottle and peered his eye through the bottle's opening hole, he instantly noticed the bottle was empty. Out of frustration and anger, he threw the bottle to the floor. The bottle fell onto a thick shaggy rug and did not shatter. Rick now had to drag his body to the kitchen sink where the running tap water would be his salvation instead. While Rick stood by the sink to quench his thirst, the indigo-blue bottle that was left lying on the shaggy rug began to release a grayish-purple smoke from its opening. The smoke slowly leaked out of the bottle and began to float into the air. At the start, the smoke appeared thin; but the longer it escaped into the air, the larger it grew. It wasn't until the smoke floated above the table and stood as high as the ceiling did Rick finally notice it. Startled, Rick backed himself toward his stove, trying to process what he was seeing. At first Rick thought, *Fire!* But there was no smell to the smoke that would usually indicate there was a fire, and there was no heat originating from that area as well. When he drew closer to the smoke's origin, he could finally see where it was coming from—the blue bottle. As the smoke engulfed the room, Rick could see a figure of a person appearing behind the smoke. The figure was obscure at first, but after a few minutes, it began to grow in shape and in distinction. It was the shape of a woman.

"Can this be?" said the woman, looking at the dispersing smoke around her.

Rick stood in silence as he clearly began to see a woman draped in a black cloak. The woman's face was pale white, and her lips were black as coal. Her hair was long and jet-black. What Rick noticed the most about her black hair were the bright-purple highlights that fell on each side of her face. There was nothing of beauty about her; however, Rick could sense an aura of power.

"Who are you?" Rick finally asked.

"Me? You ask who I am?" said the woman.

Rick noticed the woman's accent as she spoke; however, he could not place its origin. His closest guess was of European, but to determine the region, he was not that worldly or educated.

"My name is Rick," he said.

The woman nodded and agreed to share her identity, "I am Zara. Dark mistress of Avalon. Tell me, Rick, of your magic?" asked Zara.

"Magic? Avalon? I am sorry, I don't have magic, and what is an Avalon? And how did you get into that bottle?" asked Rick in bewilderment.

Zara pondered Rick's reply, trying to deduce how she could have been freed from her prison after all these centuries. "If you have no magic, then you must be an immortal, is it true?" asked Zara.

"Why do you ask?" questioned Rick.

"Because no mere human could open the cork from the bottle and release me from my longtime imprisonment. Only someone with magic or immortality could do such a thing. You did this, so tell me, who really are you, Rick?" said Zara with a stare that penetrated through Rick down to his core.

"I am human during the day, and at night, I transform into an animal, a wolf," confessed Rick.

"Hmm. So, you are immortal. I am intrigued by you, Rick. I know of this curse you speak of," said Zara.

"You do? How?" asked Rick eagerly.

"The curse was created by magic long, long ago. And it can only be undone by magic still," said Zara.

"What kind of magic?" asked Rick.

"Magic that I do," said Zara.

"Are you saying that you can make me human again and remove my curse?" asked Rick.

"Yes, I can do. But I will need something to help me," said Zara.

"What do you need?" asked Rick eagerly.

"I will need one of the artifacts that once belonged to the Vault of Avalon. It is the Jade Crystal. There's one person who will know of it," said Zara.

"Okay, so where is this person and how do we get it?" asked Rick.

"I feel she is close. I can sense her magic," said Zara.

"Then we need to find her so I can be normal again," said Rick with conviction.

"Wait, so you wish to be human again? Why?" asked Zara curiously.

"Every night, I chain myself to the wall so I cannot escape and harm others. I am always afraid of what I will do when my animal side awakens," confessed Rick.

"I see. Have you ever thought of your curse as a gift with the potential for great power?" asked Zara.

Rick gave Zara a curious glance. "What do you mean?"

"Seems to me you have lived only as a prisoner to your human side. Your animal side deserves to be free to use its instincts as any animal. What you need and don't have is a master to help guide you," said Zara.

"I'm sorry but I don't like taking orders if that's what you mean?" said Rick sternly.

"You misunderstand me. I mean to say master to your animal side and partner to your human side. You see?" said Zara.

Rick was starting to understand Zara and what she had to offer. She was offering an alliance. It was an alliance that could give him what he always wanted or something he never dreamed of having. At this point, it was an offer he could not refuse.

"I understand now. But how can I be sure you will be able to control my animal side when I transform? What if I harm you?" asked Rick.

"Hahaha," bellowed Zara. "I fear not your animal side. Your animal side will not harm me," said Zara.

"How can you be so sure?" questioned Rick.

"I am sure. But you need to see for yourself," said Zara.

Zara began to rub her hands together and started chanting. Rick watched as Zara moved closer to him, and as she was an arm's length away, without warning she thrust her palm into Rick's chest. Rick fell to the floor and, within seconds, transformed into his wolf form. Zara had forced a transformation during the daytime.

Rick stood on all fours in his living before Zara.

"You have human eyes, I see. Now look at me with them," commanded Zara.

The wolf lifted his head and stared at his new master. When Zara's gaze met with the animal's, human Rick beneath the animal could hear Zara talk to him, and in return, he could communicate back. And as they spoke within their minds, the animal's rage turned docile. For the first time while in animal form, he could communicate with someone. Rick knew from this point on whatever Zara wanted, he would abide by; he was now hers to command. Then with another thrust of her palm into the animal's fur, Rick transformed back into his man self.

"Now, are you sure?" asked Zara.

Rick nodded.

"Good. We are agreed. Now you must rest while I discover this new land—this new time for myself," said Zara.

"I don't think it is a good idea to go outside looking like you do. If you run into people, you could scare them," said Rick.

"Having people fear me is nothing uncommon. If people fear you, you have power over them. When people fear you, they are weak and easily controlled. If I am to rule this land, instilling fear will be necessary," said Zara.

Rick watched as Zara stepped back from him and crouched to the floor. Her cloak covered her body, and he could hear her chant more words he could not understand. As the chanting grew louder the cloak's material began to transform, and Zara's size began to reduce. The cloak's black wool-like material shape shifted into feathers, and Zara herself followed by transforming into a large black bird right before Rick's eyes. Rick watched as the bird looked back at him. and as clear as he could hear his thoughts, he heard Zara speak to him in his mind. He opened one of his windows and lifted Zara to the windowsill. Just as the bird was about to soar into the blue sky, Rick asked it, "Where are you going?"

Without a voice but only words in his mind, she replied to him, "I've got to find her."

Chapter

14

The camp was in shambles, but we managed to find a tent that luckily was not shredded to pieces from the animal attacks. We used the tent as shelter to rest for the night. As day broke, we all rose to get an early start home. The hole that kept Sam safe remained intact during the night. I could see that my father couldn't hold back any longer what he wanted to say last night.

"Emily, what happened last night and what you did, that was magic, right?" asked my father.

"Yes, it was," I replied.

"This is what Serena was telling you about?" he added.

"Yes, but at the time I first told you, I was still learning about what I can do. Ever since then, Serena has been helping me develop, and I can feel my powers grow stronger slowly," I said.

"How have you been communicating with Serena?" asked Cy.

"There have been many times, but all were done through my reflection. If I can see myself, then I can see and talk to her," I said.

"I see. So, if we can somehow create an image of you and somehow be able to see what you see then..." Cy paused with a pensive look.

"Where are you going with this Cy?" asked my father.

"Hmmm. Well, I think I might have a way we can also witness and maybe experience this communication connection between Emily and Serena. I just need to get to my lab and set it up," said Cy.

"Great! Then let's start heading back," I said.

"First, we need to check on and figure out what we should do about Sam," said my father, motioning me toward the hole.

My father called out to Sam to see if he was in fact Sam again. To our relief, Sam's voice replied in human form.

Now, I had to figure out a way to remove the roots. I began by laying my hands on the ground. Once I could see my hands glow orange, I then focused on the feeling of melting. Once I did that, the roots fell off the tree trunks. Now, all I had to do next was levitate the trunks away from the hole, which was easily done since I used the same energy and magic that put them there in the first place.

"Um, I am going to need some clothes before I come out," said Sam, noticing his freedom.

"Here you go. Luckily, we kept the rope secured to the tree," said Cy as he threw down some clothes to Sam. We waited for Sam to dress and finally climb out of the hole. When Sam finally emerged, I noticed the dirt on his face and arms. And also noticed he was not limping.

"How's your ankle?" I asked remembering its injury.

"Oh yeah, I completely forgot about that. Looks and feels fine," said Sam, rotating his ankle as a test.

"Hmm. I wonder if the transformation from human to animal helps with that healing process. Interesting…," added Cy.

"Consider me your new science project, Cy. I am willing to find out as much as I can about this curse," said Sam.

"From what I know of it, you are definitely not a threat to us during the daytime. So, let's start heading back home. The sooner we can get home, the sooner Cy can get to work on both you and Emily," said my father.

"Oh, whatever happened to Rick?" asked Sam.

"Wolf Rick ended up running off into the woods. So, I am going on the assumption that human Rick is still alive and maybe recovering from his injuries," said Cy.

"Funny how we came out here to find a wolf and ended up finding two," said Sam.

"Well, we will be helping you stay safe for your change tonight, that's for sure," I said.

"What do we do about Rick?" asked Cy.

"Rick told me he has a way of not harming others when he changes," added Sam.

"Then how did this happen to you if he was so careful?" I asked.

"Rick said I was a mistake that should not have happened. It was a drunken night mistake. He wanted to make amends by taking me under his wing and teaching me how to live with this curse. But I was too angry at the time to really listen," said Sam.

"At this point, we need to regroup and get more answers. If Cy can figure out this communication connect between Serena and Emily, as well as work on creating a secure area for Sam, I can also do some research on the curse. I think I have some old books that will help," said my father.

"Got to love it when a plan comes together," I said.

We gathered all our belongings and broke camp. The hike back to the ranger's station was going to be at least a few hours, which my father deduced would get us home by midday, especially since we got an early start. During our hike back, I realized it was my chance to really talk to Sam now that I knew about his secret and he knew about mine.

"So, you are a wolf, huh?" I asked.

"Yeah, I really wanted to tell you," said Sam.

"So, I am guessing that is what Rick warned you about?" I asked.

"Yup, and I was wrong to listen to Rick. I was just so unsure," confessed Sam.

"Forget about it. I get it. Don't worry," I said casually.

"So, you really do have magic," Sam added. "You know, I still have the bruises from it," he said with a grin.

We both smiled at each other, understanding each other's own discoveries.

"How much of last night to you remember?" I asked.

"I remember everything. But the two most terrifying moments were when I transformed in the hole. And when I lost control of my anger and the animal side of me took over. I was so afraid of hurting you," said Sam.

"I could sense you were there behind the all the fur when you came out of the hole. I saw your eyes and just knew," I said. "Sam, I promise

I will not let you hurt anyone," I added, stopping Sam from his hike and facing him.

"Okay, then I also want you to promise me that if my animal side ever gets out of control, that you will do everything in your power to stop me. Even if that means ending my life," said Sam with such seriousness I was afraid to want to commit to that promise.

"You really don't mean that," I said.

"Yes, I do. Promise me, Emily! This curse cannot continue. It has to end with me," pleaded Sam.

I saw the desperation in his eyes, and I knew it would certainly wound his soul deeply if he ever ended someone else's life.

I lowered my face and replied. "I promise,"

Sam raised my head up with his finger and looked into my eyes. "Thank you, Emily," he said.

Even though I may have mustered a smile to his gratitude, I prayed deep down that I would never have to honor that promise.

"Get moving you two," hollered my father from a short distance ahead.

Once we heard that, we both quickened our pace to catch up to my father and Cy.

During the next few feet of travelling, I couldn't grasp the reality of my promise to Sam. I don't think I even wanted to face it. It was a burden too heavy on my own heart. I suppose my sullen look caught my father's attention as he moved his way over to my side and wrapped his huge arm around my shoulders.

"I see you are still wearing those old ratty boots of yours," said my father pointing to my feet.

"You know they are my lucky boots. It's hard for me to give something up I get so attached to," I said.

"So true. Speaking of attachments, I can't help but notice how well you and Sam are getting along. Honestly, I like the kid, minus the whole wolf thing," said my father with a smile.

"Yeah, he's turning out to be a really good friend," I said.

"Being friends is good. As your father, I can approve friendship. There is so much that can grow out of something so special," said my father.

"What are you saying?" I asked.

"What I am saying is that I can see how you both care about each other. And the more you spend time together, the more that compassion will grow and develop," said my father.

"I remember what it was like when you and Mom first met. Over time you, both became inseparable," I said.

"Yes, that is true. Before your mother came into my life, I knew nothing of love and friendship. And as the years went on, I started to learn more about trust and family. Emily, you already have these qualities embedded in your own soul. You will change Sam's life just like your mother changed mine," said my father.

I looked up at my father and then buried my face into his chest, feeling comforted by his words but also saddened by what I needed to tell him or ask him next.

"Father, what was it like knowing you were going to outlive those you care about?" I asked.

"You mean when I was immortal?" he asked with a puzzled tone.

"Yes," I replied.

"Well, it was hard. When you have something so precious in your life, you always want to be able to protect it or be with it forever. Why do you ask?" asked my father.

"The gift of having Serena's magic also comes with the price: my mortality," I said, looking up at my father's face to see if he understood.

My father stopped his pace and put both of his hands on my shoulders, "So, you are now an immortal?" said my father.

"Yes," I replied.

"This is a great burden on you. You do realize that, right?" stated my father.

"I know. When Serena first told me, I instantly thought of you. I realize what I am taking on is going to be a huge responsibility and the thought of one day not having you, mom, Cy, and Ms. Pike around in my life does scare me a little. I think that's why I am telling you this now," I confessed.

"Emily, we live a unique life. Sometimes, in our efforts to help others, it puts our lives in danger. I almost lost Cy to a wolf last night. And your mother, I am sure worries about me more now that I am mortal. So I guess what I am saying is we could lose the people we love any day, at any time. And even you, although you have immortality what I have learned about the mystic world is that there is always someone else with more power or strength that can destroy you," said my father.

"So, whether you are mortal or immortal, you are still vulnerable?" I questioned.

"Yes. And it's fear that makes us vulnerable the most. Whatever makes us afraid will also make us fail. When you can let go of that fear, you will find your inner power," said my father.

"How do I do that?" I asked.

"You have to trust yourself," said my father as he gently leaned down to kiss my forehead.

I closed my eyes and felt his tenderness on my forehead. As I watched him begin to walk the trail toward the others, his wisdom left me in awe. I understood what he was trying to say, but I also hadn't lived centuries of a lifetime that he has to have gained such knowledge either. I can only hope that one day, his words to me at this point will prove to be true. And as we continued our trek toward the ranger's station, each of us were lost in our own thoughts.

Chapter

15

Within the clouds Zara soared over the trees and the land below. She surveyed this new world before her, and what she discovered was that there were many differences from the world she once knew. This world had stranger objects that moved on circular mechanisms between white and yellow lines. And its castles and fortresses stood taller, grander, and in abundance. When she finally had the opportunity to encounter the people of this time and place, she decided to so see if they have changed as well. Taking a break from her flight, Zara perched on a tree branch; she peered down at four strangers who wore clothing that appeared unfamiliar, and she wondered why these humans had large bags over their back as they travelled through the forest. Nevertheless, the four humans below her would be enough to begin with. Zara flew off the branch and landed a few feet in front of the humans onto the ground so to have time to transform before she approached them. Zara watched as the hikers continued to walk the grassy path, unaware of her presence.

"So, whose bright idea was it to take this trail?" said one of the females from the group.

"I think it was Jack's, as usual," said another female voice.

"Hey, in my defense, I didn't hear anyone else volunteering their thoughts on the matter," said a male voice, known to the group as Jack.

"It's cool, Jack, I don't mind your scenic route. The gals just like giving you a hard time," said the last male voice in the group with a chuckle.

"Thanks, man!" said Jack, giving the other male a fist bump to signify their male bond.

Just as the group were about to follow the bend in the path, Zara walked out of the bushes, catching them by surprise.

"Whoa! Who are you?" said Jack, stepping back, holding up his arms, bringing the rest of the members of the group to a halt.

Zara looked at the group closely. "I am Zara. What names do each of you go by?" said Zara.

"Well, I'm Jack. And this is Brandon, Melanie, and Kristen," said Jack, pointing to each member of his group.

"Are you lost, ma'am?" asked Brandon.

"No, but I am new to this place. And I am looking for someone," said Zara.

"Is the person you are looking for lost?" asked Melanie.

"The person I seek is lost from me, yes. So, I need help to find them," said Zara.

"Do you know where you last saw them?" asked Kristen.

"We can help you look for them," said Jack.

Zara could see their innocence. And the kindness of their gesture would be a weakness she could easily prey upon.

"Yes, you will help me," said Zara as she led the group into the woods and off the grassy path.

The group looked at each other in hesitation at first and then gave a final glance over at Jack.

"We said we would help," said Jack, shrugging his shoulders and motioning the others to follow Zara.

The group continued to follow Zara deeper into the woods. The more each member asked Zara questions about where they were heading, Zara simply replied, "Not far now," and continued to walk ahead of them.

"Jack, we are really far from the trail. Maybe we should just let the park rangers help her find the person she is looking for," said Brandon.

"Yeah, Jack, I have a bad feeling about her," said Kristen.

Jack quietly agreed with the group and decided to speak up.

"Hey, maybe we should get the park ranger to help you with your search for your friend. I mean, there is not much we can do if we don't know who we are looking for and where they are. We are just casual hikers and don't really know the area that well," said Jack.

Zara continued to walk a few more paces, ignoring Jack's comment. She came to the base of a small hill and looked upon it as the place she could begin. Zara walked up the incline of hill and finally turned toward the group and looked down at their young worried faces.

"Why are we here?" asked Melanie.

"Look, lady, I'm sorry, but I think we should leave and head back to the trail before we lose any more daylight," said Brandon, growing agitated.

Zara still said nothing but continued to look down at the group and watched as their emotions began to unravel. Then she started to chant.

"Jack, I think we need to get out of here, man," said Brandon.

"Yeah, Jack, this woman is definitely scaring me. What is she doing?" said Kristen.

"All right, guys, let's get out of here," said Jack, leading the group away from Zara.

But Zara's chant grew louder, and as she continued to chant, tree roots broke from the ground and grew up simultaneously. Each moving root began connecting to one another as if creating a chain-link fence around the group. Everywhere each member turned, it was being closed off by the root-like fence.

"What is going on?" yelled Jack.

Both Melanie and Kristen screamed.

"Dude, this is not good. There is no way out," yelled Brandon, trying to force his way through the wooden barricade.

"There is no escape for you now," said Zara, walking toward the caged group.

"Why are you doing this?" cried Kristen.

"What do you want from us?" asked Jack.

"I want what I always wanted. You will all to help me find someone," said Zara.

"Okay, we will, just don't hurt us," pleaded Jack.

"Silly boy, my intention is not to hurt you. I need you all," said Zara with a devilish smile.

"If you don't plan on hurting us, then what do you plan on doing with us?" asked Jack, now face-to-face with Zara against the wooden fence.

Zara smiled and rubbed her hands together and began a whispering chant. The others who stood back from the fence watched as Jack and Zara exchanged words. Zara's chant caught Jack off guard, and as she moved closer to the fence, she thrust her palm into Jack's chest through a small opening in the fence. Jack fell back onto the ground, and before all his friends, he began to convulse.

"Jack!" yelled Melanie.

"What did you do to him?" pleaded Kristin.

Jack turned over on to his chest and crouched to the ground, trembling uncontrollably, releasing his backpack from his shoulders. His friends attempted to rush to his side to help until they heard Zara's warning, "I would not get too close to him if I were you," she said.

"We have to help him! It looks like he is dying!" cried Melanie.

"Step back to the fence and let the magic be completed," said Zara, with authority.

The group had no choice but to move toward the edge of the fence and witness what Jack was transforming into.

"Jack, man, are you okay? Jack!" yelled Brandon.

"Brandon look! Jack's hands—" shouted Kristen, pointing at Jack.

"Oh, man, are those claws coming out of his fingers?" shouted Brandon.

Both girls turned their heads away from the rest of the transformation. Brandon, however, could not look away and wanted to see the change to the end. Once the claws from Jack's fingers and the fur coming from Jack's skin and the finally the fangs that grew from Jack's teeth came into full form, Brandon could now see the truth. Zara had turned Jack into an animal, a wolf. When the girls finally looked back to see what Jack had turned into, they both screamed and hid behind Brandon as the wolf glared at them and growled. Once Zara saw Jack complete his transformation, she called to him but not with spoken words. Like she had done with Rick, Jack, even in animal form, could hear Zara's words call to him in his head. The wolf looked at Zara instantly, and when Zara met the animal's gaze, his temperament changed from viciousness to compliance.

"This is how you can be of help to me," said Zara as she began to rub her hands together again and moved toward the rest of the group, who were all pressed against the fence.

As the wolf kept the group at bay by the fence, Zara thrust her palm into each of them one at a time, allowing the magic that turned Jack into what he had become now work to do the same on his friends. Outside the links of the wooden prison, Zara watched as the remaining youngsters began their transformation. Zara smiled in confidence knowing that soon, she would have the beginning of her new army.

Chapter

16

It was midday, and as my father had predicted, we reached the ranger's station. The Jeep had remained in the same parking spot, and the ranger's cabin—once examined by Cy—was empty. It appeared to all of us that Rick was nowhere in sight. One by one, we climbed into our seats after loading what we carried into the back of the Jeep. My father fired up the engine, and we were off down the road toward home.

"Emily, tell me more about your connection with Serena?" asked Cy.

"What do you want to know?" I replied.

"Well, you said that you communicate through your reflection and that you have done it many times during the trip. How were you finding your reflection?" asked Cy.

"At first it was through my bathroom mirror. And then I did it through a small puddle in the forest," I said, trying to recall the third way.

"You also did it on your phone, remember?" added Sam.

"Yes, that's it. I used my phone to get my digital reflection and connected with Serena that way too," I said.

"So, you were able to connect with Serena digitally?" asked Cy.

"Yeah, I was surprised it worked too. But Serena did say that all I needed to do was find my reflection and call out her name," I said.

"Perfect! If you can see her digitally, then I can create a link for us to see and hear what you hear, Emily. My lab will have everything I need," concluded Cy.

"What about me? How are we going to keep me caged during my change tonight?" asked Sam.

"I think I have a solution for that as well. Again, it's all in my lab." said Cy.

"Are you talking about the shield?" whispered my father to Cy.

"Yes, we can slightly have it modified," said Cy.

"Were you thinking of room 42?" added my father.

"Perhaps, but I did upgrade the keypad to work with any room," said Cy.

"So, you made it portable?" asked my father.

"Yes, I did. I thought it would come in useful one day," said Cy.

"Looks like your timing is perfect as usual," added my father.

Sam looked at my father and Cy in confusion.

Then Sam turned to me, "Are they always like that?" Sam asked.

I laughed, knowing exactly what Sam was referring too. "Don't worry, my father and Cy have a way of communicating where only they know what they are talking about. I have learned to just go with it and trust it," I said with a smile.

Sam smiled back. "So long as they are working out a plan, I'm all good with it," said Sam.

"With Cy, you can bet a plan is always in the works even when we don't realize we need one," I said to Sam.

Just as the drive was turning out to be as content and uneventful, the satellite phone my mother gave to my father started to ring.

—⚊🐛⚊—

The mansion was quiet while the others were gone. Ellie and Ms. Pike spent the morning when the group was gone catching up on the adventures from Ms. Pike's vacation. The remaining hours for Ellie were spent relaxing, eating, and occasionally writing. Ellie knew her family would be back some time the next day, but she still had her scheduled doctor's visit for the afternoon she needed to go to. Ms. Pike offered to accompany and drive Ellie, but Ellie stubbornly refused the offer and wanted to drive herself. Ellie's drive into town was pleasant, and when she arrived at her doctor's office, she was hoping for the usual baby news and updates from her doctor. However, what she didn't anticipate was an unexpected casual encounter that would eventually become a dangerous threat to her.

"Ellie, everything is on track for you," said her doctor.

"Good. I know it's still early, but I am really ready to pop this baby out," said Ellie, jokingly.

The doctor laughed, "You are not the only pregnant woman who has said that to me once or twice a day," said the doctor.

Ellie shrugged her shoulders and chuckled.

"For our next visit, I would prefer you not driving here. I see you are alone today. Is there someone who can drive you next time? Or do I need to make a house call?" said the doctor.

"My family is just out of town for the day, and I wanted to make the drive myself. Next visit, there will be someone who will drive me. I promise, Doc," said Ellie.

"Okay, I will hold you to that. I don't anticipate any problems for you between now and our next visit. So, keep doing what you are doing," said the doctor.

"Thanks, Doc," said Ellie, getting up to leave the office.

Ellie arrived at her car and noticed something so odd. On the hood of her car quietly stood a bird. A big black bird that just simply sat there and looked out at the traffic and buildings. As Ellie drew closer, she could see that the bird was not bothered by the sounds of the people passing by. *That's so strange,* she thought. What was also peculiar was what Ellie noticed on the side of the bird's body.

Ellie carefully crept to the driver's side door and slid into the driver's seat as to not attract the bird's attention just in case it was going to attack her. Safely in the car, Ellie honked her horn to scare the bird off the hood. The bird did not move. Ellie honked her horn again. The bird simply turned its head toward her and stared. The bird cocked its head to the side, unable to release its gaze on Ellie. Then Ellie tried to shoo it away with her hands from within the car. Still, the bird did not move. After several failed attempts to remove the bird from her hood, Ellie decided to just start the engine and maybe the bird will just fly away on its own. When the bird heard the engine rev, it then decided to move, but in a direction that Ellie did not anticipate. The bird began to walk toward Ellie's windshield. As the bird reached the windshield, it walked up the glass and peered down at Ellie. The bird could see Ellie in full view, full pregnant view. Then without warning, the bird with big black wings and a purple stripe along its body leaped off Ellie's car. It was finally gone. Ellie shifted her car in gear and drove toward home with an ominous feeling too difficult to ignore. Ellie took the usual route home without even noticing she was being followed. Ellie's stalker waited until she was about five minutes from her driveway. The unwanted stalker flew by Ellie's windshield, barely missing the glass; however, the sudden distraction was more than enough to startle Ellie. Ellie screamed. The car veered off the road as screeching tires skid the car off to the side and down into a deep ditch. The descending movement of the car onto the steep slope caused Ellie to hit her head on the steering wheel just before the airbags deployed, leaving her unconscious yet still strapped in her seat belt. The impact into the bottom of the ditch left the front end crushed and smoking. Along the bottom and on each slope of the ditch, tall dry grass blades grew, surrounding Ellie's car. At the bottom of the ditch, Ellie's car was completely hidden from the road. Any chance to be found would prove difficult unless they knew exactly where her car landed. The only witness to the accident was the one who caused it. The culprit sat perched on a nearby fence post, surveying the damage she had caused. Satisfied at what she accomplished, she flapped her big black wings again and flew off toward the trees.

On the other end of the satellite phone was Ms. Pike. Cy was the one who initially picked up the call.

"Ms. Pike, this is Cy. What is the nature of your call?" asked Cy as he adjusted the phone so everyone could listen in on the call.

"Daniel!" called out Ms. Pike. "Ellie left about two hours ago for her doctor's appointment, and she hasn't come home yet."

"Did you call the doctor's office? Maybe she is still there," said my father.

"I did. They said she left about an hour ago. I also tried calling her cell phone. Daniel, she is not picking up," said Ms. Pike, trying to contain her panic.

Concerned, I tried calling my mother's phone as well. No answer.

"Father, Ms. Pike is right. I can't get a hold of Mom either. This is not like her," I said.

"Hang tight, Ms. Pike, we are almost to the house," said my father.

After talking to Ms. Pike, my father drove faster to arrive at the house sooner. We all ran out of the Jeep to find Ms. Pike standing on the front steps waiting for us.

"Daniel! Thank goodness you are here," said Ms. Pike.

"Anything new?" asked my father.

"No. Ellie is still not home, and I am really worried about her. I knew I should have driven her, but she insisted on driving herself," said Ms. Pike.

"It's okay, Ms. Pike. My mom can be stubborn. We will find her," I reassured.

"Oh dearie. What if something terrible has happened to her?" said Ms. Pike with a look of worry.

"Did Mom say if she was going anywhere after her appointment?" I asked.

"No, she was going to come straight home after her appointment because she knew you all would be back, and she wanted to be home," said Ms. Pike.

Cy had already made his way to his lab to map out the route Mom would take on her way home. My father joined him as they tried to retrace Mom's whereabouts.

Ms. Pike, Sam, and I stood by the front door. When I realized the door was still open, I moved to close it. Just as I had the door half shut, Sam grabbed my hand, stopping me from finishing the motion.

"Do you smell that?" asked Sam.

"Smell what?" I replied.

Sam opened the door, sniffed the air, and ran out onto the driveway. I followed him.

"Sam, what are you doing?" I asked.

"I know where your mom is," said Sam.

"What? How?" I asked.

"Ms. Pike said she was driving, right?" said Sam.

"Yes, but—" I said unable to finish what I had to say.

"Follow me," said Sam as he ran off toward the road.

"Sam!" I cried out. Having no choice, I followed and ran in the same direction as Sam.

Sam was a few steps ahead of me. When we reached the end of the driveway, Sam continued down one of the main roads. I couldn't figure out what he was doing. And I couldn't understand why we continued to run down the road, but every gut instinct within led me to just trust his lead. We ran for a good ten minutes until Sam stopped. When I finally caught up to him, he was standing in the middle of the road. Where we both stood was a lonely strip of road, which had on each side houses with driveways that ran eighty feet from the road. The houses themselves were pushed so far back from the road. The only thing that stood between the properties and the road were very large ditches.

Sam stiffed the air again as I looked around at the road.

"The smell is right here," said Sam.

"What?" I asked.

"Gasoline," said Sam as he walked to the edge of the ditch. "Emily! Call your father," shouted Sam.

I ran to Sam's side, and as I reached the edge, I could see the taillight from my mother's car buried in the tall grass. I quickly grabbed my phone from my pocket and called my father.

"Emily? Where are you?" said my father, picking up my call.

"We found Mom. Her car is in a ditch a few feet from the house, on County Road 17. Hurry!" I shouted.

"OK. Sit tight. Cy and I are on our way. Emily, don't you or Sam do anything until we get there," said my father.

"I'm going to leave my phone on, so you can track it," I said.

I left my phone on, and I ran back over to Sam.

"They are coming, Sam. Nice work," I said.

"It's not good enough unless we can find a way to get her out," said Sam, staring down at the ditch.

"My father said to wait until they get here," I urged.

But I knew that look in Sam. He wasn't going to wait for backup.

"Emily, I can smell blood. Your mother is hurt. My concern is for the baby," said Sam.

Smell blood? I thought.

Regardless of whether I knew if Sam was right or not, I had to know if my mom was okay. I left my phone by the side of road for my father, and we both started to make our way to the bottom of the ditch. The tall grassy slope made it easy to descend as we held on to the long blades on the way down. It had not rained for months, making the bottom of the ditch drier than usual. Instead of a bed of water and a muddy base, the car's front end collided into a more solid grassy wall, causing the impact to be more severe. As we drew closer to the car, I started to smell the gasoline Sam was referring to. Wondering how he smelt it all the way from the house was intriguing. The car went front end first into the ditch. The front window, luckily, was still intact and so were the side windows. When we finally reached the car, I called out to my mother.

"Mom!" I yelled.

Sam and I moved to the driver's side and saw my mother lying there, unconscious with the air bags deployed in front of her. Her head was bleeding like Sam had said. But when I could see that she was not moving, I started to panic.

"Mom! It's Emily, wake up," I said banging on her window.

Sam tried to open the door, but it was locked or maybe jammed.

"Sam, we have to get in there," I said urgently.

"Find something to break the window with," said Sam.

I searched the grounds for something to use, but I couldn't find anything big enough to break a car window. Any of the big rocks were buried into the ground around the grass.

"Sam I can't find anything," I cried out.

Sam heard my cry but also heard another sound coming from beneath the car. When I saw Sam bend down to the ground, I had to know what he was doing, so I followed to the ground as well.

"Sam, what is that?" I asked, noticing something electrical coming from beneath the front of car.

"Emily, that is a live wire. The car's impact must have caused it," said Sam.

"With the live wire underneath the car, we should be safe from the sparks, right?" I asked.

"Yes, but we still need to get your mom out of here. A spark is only dangerous if it comes into contact with something flammable. We still need to hurry," said Sam.

Sam continued to pry the driver's side door open. He pulled and pushed, hoping to release it from the jam. When I noticed Sam's success at freeing the door from its jam, I joined him, and we both pulled with all our strength to open the door completely.

"We did it!" I cheered in relief, moving to examine my mother's injuries.

"How is she?" asked Sam.

"Mom, it's Emily, can you hear me?" I said, trying to awaken my mother from her sleepy state.

"Emily," whispered my mother.

"Mom, Sam and I are here. And we are going to get you out," I said.

"Where am I?" said my mother, still weak in speech.

"Your car went off the road. Father and Cy are on their way. Just stay awake. Stay with me, Mom," I said, cradling my mother's head in my arms, dabbing the blood on her forehead.

Sam was able to release my mother's seat belt, and with gentle ease, we lifted my mother out of the driver's seat and onto the ground. I examined her wounds and was relieved to see that the only wound was the small scrap on her head. She was able to move her arms and her legs but felt too dizzy to stand.

"My mom is stable. That's a good thing. We just need to wait for my father and Cy," I said.

"Wait," said Sam.

Sam began to sniff around the car and once again bent down to the ground.

"Emily, we need to move your mom now!" demanded Sam.

"Why? What is it?" I asked in concern.

"I think while we were forcing the door open, we also caused a leak in the gas tank. Emily, gasoline is slowly leaking from beneath the car and moving toward the spark," said Sam as calm as possible to avoid causing a panic.

Despite Sam's calming words, I did start to panic. We were at the bottom of a very deep ditch with no way to elevate ourselves and my mother out of it. I could not even call my father because I left my phone on the road so we would be tracked faster.

"Emily, we need to at least get your mom and us as far away from the car as possible," said Sam.

I agreed and whispered to my mother to grab on to Sam and myself to try to stand. My mother lifted her arms and wrapped them around each of our shoulders. She slowly lifted to a stance for a few minutes and then collapsed to the ground.

"I'm too dizzy, honey. I'm sorry I can't stand," said my mom.

"Sam," I said, looking at him for another option.

Just as we tried to figure out another option, the spark beneath the car started to grow; and the gasoline had already made its way toward it, creating a small fire at the car's hood. Sam and I knew it would be just a matter of time before the rest of gasoline traveling downhill would pool by the live wire. And once that happened, any flame that had already started could lead to more combustible danger.

Sam instantly scooped my mother up in his arms and decided to carry her away from the car himself. I watched as Sam's cheeks blew in and out as a weightlifter would do preparing to lift weights. He managed to get my mother off the ground, but her added pregnancy weight was going to be a struggle for him.

"You got her?" I asked.

"Yes, just move. We need to clear this car now. The gasoline is getting close," Sam said, carrying my mother in his arms.

We quickly began our escape away from the dangers that loomed. Sam ran ahead of me with my mother, and I ran behind. As our steps drew us farther from the wreckage, the more the flames grew until the front hood of the car was engulfed. We had created some distance but needed to get farther. Sam and I ran as fast as we could until a pair of the buried rocks stopped my momentum. I had accidently fallen and got my foot caught between two rocks hidden by the tall dry grass.

"Sam!" I called out.

Sam stopped and turned around, "Emily!" he yelled back in concern.

Just as Sam witnessed my fall, a sudden explosion came from the car. I tucked my head to the ground in hopes to shield myself from any debris. Luckily, I was far enough from the blast's range. But some of the flaming debris landed on the dry grass, suddenly causing it to flash into a creeping inferno. I struggled to free my boot from its wedge between the rocks, but it would not move. My foot was completely wedged in. I needed to get my boot off. Frantically, I worked on getting my laces undone. I watched as the flames drew closer, consuming every blade of dry grass in its path. I finally had my laces undone. I tried to wiggle my foot free, but I didn't have the leverage to get my foot out of my boot.

"Come on!" I screamed, still trying to pull myself free.

"Emily, I got you," said Sam as he put his arms underneath my armpits, giving the leverage I needed.

"Sam, where's my mom?" I asked.

"She's safe. You're almost there," said Sam, pulling me free.

My foot was finally free. I scurried to my feet with my one boot.

"Let's go. The fire is spreading," said Sam.

"Go where? The fire is going to move along the bottom of the ditch," I said.

"Then we just stay ahead of it," said Sam.

I agreed with Sam and kept moving forward. Sam picked my mother back up from the ground he laid her on and continued along the ditch. I followed. We were able to stay a few feet ahead of the spreading fire but also so far from our original location. I wondered if my father and Cy would know where we had gone.

"Emily, what is that?" said Sam looking ahead.

"That's a driveway," I said referring to the wall of concrete ahead.

"There must be a drainage system that runs through it, right?" Sam asked.

"Yes, there usually is," I replied.

"We can hide in there and use it to protect us from the flames," said Sam, now coughing from the blowing smoke.

"Okay," I said in agreement also feeling the taste of smoke in my throat.

I worried that as Sam and I were feeling the effects of the blowing smoke, so would my mom. And just as I finished the thought, I heard my mom begin to cough. Sam tried his best to cover her mouth with his chest, protecting her from inhaling it into her lungs. Sam was sure that once we got to the drainage area, we would be fine; we would be safe. Little did we know the drainage would not be our salvation. When we reached the wall, any hope Sam had held to keep us safe faded. The drainage system was not what we had expected. Yes, it used to have water flow through them but only water and anything the size of a possum. The openings were not big enough for us to fit through. The fire was spreading not only along the bottom of the ditch but also along the slopes. We were trapped.

When Daniel and Cy reached the location of Emily's phone, they had just heard the blast coming from the ditch below. Daniel ran to the side of the road and peered down toward the ditch.

"There's the car," shouted Daniel.

"You mean that was the car. Where is everyone?" asked Cy.

"Cy, the ditch is becoming a giant fire trap. If they are still down there, they would have to stay ahead of the smoke and fire," said Daniel.

"But which way did they go?" asked Cy.

Daniel tried to see through the smoke any evidence of tracks, but the fire had covered up everything near the car, and the rising smoke blocked his distant view. Daniel looked ahead to the left; nothing. He then looked ahead to the right and barely caught a glimpse of something small yet familiar lying by some rocks just before it got caught up in the flames. Daniel now knew the direction they went in. Daniel quickly motioned for Cy to get back into the car and head farther down the road. Racing down the road, Daniel saw how the thickness of smoke had risen above the slopes. They needed to be ahead of the black clouds to see anything below.

"Cy, pull over right there," said Daniel, pointing to a pathway off the road.

Daniel knew if they were still down there, time was running out. He feared for his family's safety and prayed timing would be on his side. When Daniel got out of the car, he ran to see what was below the concrete wall. Daniel saw Sam, Emily, and an injured Ellie huddled by the corner of the wall. The fire was spreading faster than he had expected, and they had nowhere else to go. Time was not on his side. Daniel's only hope to save his family had to be something short of a miracle.

—⚬—

Sam and I did our best to shield my mother from the smoke, but we were all feeling the effects of the fumes. The heat from the flames were also growing intense.

"Sam, there is a small window to climb up that slope. You can make it," I said, pointing to an area not yet suffered from the blaze.

"No! I am not leaving you and Ellie here," said Sam.

"You have to. My father and Cy will find us, but they will need your help," I insisted.

"Stop it, Emily! I will not leave you both here. When they find us, they will find us all together," Sam demanded.

I looked at Sam then at my mother lying on the ground, looking frail and helpless. *My father will find us, but if he is getting ready for a rescue, he might just need more time,* I desperately thought as I watched the fire draw closer, slowly consuming every escapable path.

I tried to hold back my tears, but it was so hard because the overwhelming fear of losing people I cared about was becoming a reality. I bowed my head in defeat, succumbing to my emotions. I stared down at my missing boot, and in that moment, I suddenly remembered and finally understood what my father tried to tell me during our hike back from the woods.

Every living thing has energy, I thought, recalling Serena's words. *Fire is living.*

Turning toward the blaze, I closed my eyes and lifted my hands to the air to feel the heat from the flames as if I stood by a campfire. The feeling of heat filled my entire body. There was no burning pain from it though. Instead, I felt a warm sensation. I opened my eyes and saw my hands were glowing in a bright-red color. I had held the energy of the fire, and as I moved toward the flames, I pictured the hands of a ticking clock moving as it would when keeping time. Then with one focused thought, I imaged the ticking minute hand just stop. And just as this image flashed in my mind, the fire stopped building almost as if it hit an invisible wall. Standing before the fire. I could see it didn't move forward, nor did it grow; it just burned to a stagnant halt. Sam watched in awe as my magic stopped the fire from taking our lives. And to his surprise, he looked up to see ropes and harnesses being lowered down from above the concrete wall. What my father needed; I gave. What Sam lost; I now gave back. And what I needed to learn, I realized. My father needed time, Sam needed hope, and I needed to trust myself.

Chapter

17

After the events of the day, the mansion returned to its usual productive self. Sam joined Cy in his lab to work on his encasement for the night. I was on my way to my parents' room where my mother, father, and the doctor were discussing my mother's condition. Standing in the hallway, I caught some of the conversation.

"You are a very lucky woman, Ellie. The scrapes on your head seem to be the only serious injury," said the doctor.

"What about the baby?" asked my father.

"The baby is fine. The heartbeat appears steady," stated the doctor.

"Sorry, Mom, seems like my little brother or sister already shares our stubborn gene," I said, walking into the room.

"I'll take that kind of good news. Even the stubborn streak part," said my mother, trying to stay positive.

"Now, I want you to get some rest for the next few days. I am still a bit worried about your head injury and the dizzy spells you had earlier. If you feel nausea or still dizzy during the night, I want you to call me," said the doctor sternly.

"She will be on constant watch, I promise, Doc," said my father.

"Good to hear. I leave you in good hands now, Ellie. Just get some rest," said the doctor, gathering his medical tools.

My father escorted the doctor out and downstairs to the door while I stayed by my mother's bed.

"You know, if it was not for you and Sam, I can't imagine what would have happened," said my mother.

"It was actually Sam that tracked your car to the ditch," I said.

"Sam? How did he do that? From what your father said, my car could not be seen by the road," said my mother.

"That's right," I said wondering if my father told my mother about the events in the woods and Sam's new secret.

"So, how did your catch-and-cage go in the woods?" asked my mother, knowing I would have a story to tell.

"Well, funny you should ask that. It turned out to be more than a normal catch-and-cage mission," I said.

"When you say it like that, I am getting the impression you were put in danger of some kind," said my mother.

"Okay, yes, there were some moments when our lives were a bit threatened," I said, trying to hide the seriousness of the threat just to keep my mother calm and in a restful state.

"You know how I feel about hearing the truth, Emily. So you might as well tell me everything. I will get more agitated if you try and sugarcoat it," said my mother in a calm yet authoritative tone.

"Fine. In our search for the wolf that bit Sam, we soon discovered that the animal was alive and turned out to be Father's ranger friend Rick. Rick was cursed with being a human by day and an animal at night. I saw this transformation with my own eyes. It was something I had never seen before. Cy and father managed to fend off the wolf, but when we realized Rick was the wolf that bit Sam, we soon realized what that also meant as well," I said.

"It meant Sam shared the same curse," added my mother.

"Yes. I believe Sam is still Sam, but with new changes, kind of like what is happening to me," I said.

"With Sam being part animal, that could explain how he was able to track my car. His senses are growing strong. But his animal side is still the danger. Did you have to face that side of him?" asked my mother.

"Yes, we came face-to-face with that as well," I said.

"Considering you all made it back in one piece I, will assume you all managed to face that danger safely," concluded my mother.

"Yes, we did," I said, nodding my head.

"And the changes you refer to, does that have to do with your new gift?" asked my mother.

"Yes. I have learned so much since I first saw Serena in my bathroom," I added.

"I see," said my mother.

"It's true, Ellie. From what I have seen and witnessed, Emily is growing into her power," said my father, quietly creeping into the room.

My father walked up behind me and placed his hand on my shoulder. "I see you filled your mother in on our forest adventure," he said.

"She made me," I replied.

"Of course, she did," said my father with a chuckle.

"Speaking of sharing truths, how did you know how to find us? The ditch was covered in smoke," I asked my father.

My father laughed. "I spotted your ratty old boot caught in the rocks just before it caught in flames."

I smiled at him realizing his intelligence never ceased to amaze me.

"In all seriousness, I almost lost you two, and I am so grateful I didn't," said my father, reaching out for both my mother's hand and my hand to hold.

"I could say the same thing for the both of you," added my mother.

Joined in a triad of gratitude, I came to realize what makes us vulnerable also makes us strong. I felt grateful for having both my parents here with me, and it occurred to me that when faced with my immortality, quality of time spent is far more important to me than quantity.

Just as my mother was about to return to her rest, I had to know what happened to her car.

"How did your car end up off the road?" I asked.

"I don't quite know. But I think something flew by my windshield. I got startled and lost control of the car," said my mother.

"Flew by?" asked my father.

"Yes. The last thing I remember was seeing these big black wings," said my mother.

"Okay, maybe it was just a bird that flew into your car by accident," said my father.

"Maybe. Oh, and I saw the strangest thing after my doctor's appointment," said my mother with a yawn.

"What did you see?" I asked.

"I saw a big black bird with a purple stripe along its body just sitting on my car. It was so odd," said my mother as she snuggled in a resting position.

My father and I decided to leave my mother to her rest, left her room, and made our way to Cy's lab. My father and I dismissing the cause of my mother's car accident was going to be a mistake. For little did we know, as one door of threatening events closed, another slowly creeped open, giving way to even more danger for our family.

—ɯɯ—

Zara headed back to Rick's cabin with her new subjects. Rick had been resting most of the day, and when he heard Zara's call, he rose to meet her. When Rick opened the door and walked unto his porch, he watched as Zara slowly appeared from the bushes and the trees in her female form. Rick noticed how tired Zara looked as she emerged followed by four other wolves. The wolves fanned out all around her while approaching the cabin. Rick's first instinct was of fear and then turned into curiosity as he watched all the wolves obey Zara' every command.

"What do we have here? "asked Rick.

Zara looked around and smiled. "I have brought you a small army to command," said Zara, walking up the steps and moving toward the porch chair.

"Army?" asked Rick, looking puzzled.

"Yes. To rule, we need to create fear," said Zara, easing herself into the porch chair.

"Where did you get these wolves?" asked Rick.

"I made them," said Zara.

"How?" asked Rick.

"They are just like you. Human on inside. Animal outside. I choose when they be animal and when they be human," said Zara with a look of authority.

Rick recalled his forced transformation when they first met and understood what she meant. Zara's power was great. He was really starting to truly believe that now. But as for her overall plan, he still was unsure. He looked at the wolf pack that lay before him and found it strange to be around them. Although Zara controlled them, how did she want him to command them and for what? He had to know.

"Okay, so what do you want me to do with this new army of yours? How am I supposed to command them while I am human?" asked Rick.

"While you are human, I will command. When you are animal, they will follow your lead. Your lead will come from me," said Zara, still enjoying her rest on the chair.

Rick then recalled how he was able to hear Zara's voice when he was in wolf form.

"So, you are choosing to keep them as wolves, why?" asked Rick staring down at the dark mistress.

"Yes. They stay wolves to control always. But you will be human and wolf. This I will allow," said Zara, casually leaning on the chair's arm.

"Why am I allowed to go back from human to animal?" questioned Rick.

"You are needed more. You partner, remember," said Zara.

Rick saw how this alliance could be unfolding. Now the only question left was how far did he have to go to possibly sell his soul?

Zara peered at the wolves from the chair and waved her hand to them. Each wolf looked up at her and then lay on their bellies, slowly falling asleep.

"They need to rest. As do I. Tonight, we venture out," said Zara.

"And do what?" asked Rick with a perplexed look.

"When you transform tonight, we look for others to join army," said Zara.

"What exactly is your plan?" asked Rick sternly.

Zara looked at Rick with intensity. "Do others in this world know what you are?"

Rick paused curious at Zara's question. "Yes, there are. For the longest time, no one knew until recently. Why?" asked Rick.

Zara replied with another question. "Is there another like you? Both human and animal, cursed?"

"Yes, again, that has just recently happened. How do you know all this?" asked Rick, still trying to figure out Zara's true intentions.

"When I turned you into animal at first time, I saw it," said Zara.

"What are you saying?" asked Rick.

"I could see there was one just like you. Now I wish to know of him," said Zara.

"Why?" asked Rick.

"People need to fear me. Having army creates fear. Having army of beasts bring power," said Zara, intersecting her fingers and laying her connected hands on her lap.

"Why can't you just make more wolves like you did with the other ones and build that way?" asked Rick.

Zara slightly bowed her head. "My latest creation took much of my energy and power. I need Jade Crystal. But not know where it is," said Zara.

"I thought you knew someone who knew where it was?" asked Rick.

"I searched for her but could not find. Only had a sense she was close. Still sense it but cannot understand why," said Zara, looking annoyed at her confusion.

"I see," said Rick.

"Good. Then we agreed. Tonight, you change and lead the pack to the one who is like you. We bring him back, and he will join us," said Zara.

Rick nodded and concluded if Sam came back with them willingly, there would be no harm to the rest. Rick did not want to cause harm to Daniel and the others. But deep down, he worried about it especially under Zara's command as a wolf. Despite his worries, all Rick wanted was to become human and normal again. This want consumed him so much it seemed to outweigh his moral dilemma. It was simple: if he helped Zara get what she wanted, he in the end would get what he wanted, and nothing would get in the way of achieving that goal. Nothing!

Chapter

18

By the time my father and I joined Sam and Cy in the lab, they had already completed Sam's containment facility for the night. The room was simple with four white walls and one metal doorway. The doorway had an invisible shield that allowed anyone to see inside. Once inside, there was no way to break out, nor could anyone get in. It was secure. The only way to release the shield was by inputting one code into a digital keypad that was mounted next to the metal doorway.

"All tests have been completed. Everything is fully functional now," said Cy out loud.

"I see you both have been very busy," said my father, overhearing Cy's comment.

"How's Ellie?" asked Cy and Sam in unison.

Daniel smiled. "Ellie is good. Luckily, her injuries were not serious, and the baby is unharmed and healthy too," said my father.

Cy and Sam smiled in relief.

"My mom says thank you for what you did, Sam. She wanted to tell you in person, but the doctor wants her to get some rest," I added.

"I'm just glad to hear everything worked out," said Sam.

"So, what do we have here?" asked my father, examining the room.

"Cy is amazing. Not only has he made the room secure and impenetrable, but he also made it safe," said Sam.

"How so?" I asked.

"Not only is the invisible shield for the door but it is also coated along the four walls of the cell as well. If someone were to ram against the shield, they would simply bounce off it," added Cy.

"So, if I go animalistic while inside, I won't crack my skull against the concrete," added Sam.

"I take it those were some of the modifications we talked about," added my father.

Cy smiled, nodded in pride.

"That's great, now what about me? Have you figured out how to eavesdrop on my communications with Serena?" I asked.

"Well, funny you should ask. The modifications I had to make on the design for the brain table ended up being fewer than I initially thought," concluded Cy.

"Which means?" I added.

"Which means we can test the connection within the hour," said Cy.

"That's great!" I said, eager to begin.

"Well done, Cy, as usual," added my father.

"Wait, it gets even better," said Cy with a smirk.

"What can be better?" I asked.

"I have added these," said Cy, holding up three virtual reality visors. "So more than one person can see what Emily is seeing and hearing. Or eavesdrop as Emily put it," Cy concluded.

"Brilliant!" cheered Sam. "Does that mean I can participate too?" he asked.

"Yes! With just enough time to spare before sending you into your confinement for the night," Cy concluded.

Sam beamed with excitement while my father patted Cy on the shoulder, complimenting him on his efforts. I on the other hand rushed toward Cy and gave him the biggest hug I could give.

"So, if everyone can kindly leave my lab so I can finish, that would be great," said Cy, shrugging off the praise.

We all laughed and headed for the elevator, leaving Cy to his work.

From the elevator, my father hollered out, "Let us know when you are ready for us to come back."

"Copy that," yelled Cy just as the elevator doors finished closing.

During the elevator ride, my father decided to head to his library to do some research while Sam and I headed to what we called our happy place: the kitchen for some food.

When the doors opened, my father turned right toward his destination while Sam and I turned left toward ours.

As we came closer to the kitchen, we both stopped and looked at each other. With a slow grin on both our faces, the smell of comfort food caught our senses.

"You know what that is?" I asked.

"Of course!" said Sam.

"Apple pie!" we both said in unison while beginning our race to the kitchen.

Ms. Pike had just taken the hot apple pie out of the oven and placed it on the counter when Sam and I came running into the kitchen, giggling.

"I win!" I cheered.

"What! I let you win," said Sam, pointing his finger at me as I laughed.

Ms. Pike glanced in our direction. "I see you both got a whiff of my baking surprise," she said with a smile.

"How could we not?" I asked.

"This is why we call the kitchen our happy place," said Sam as he leaned against the counter, taking in the cinnamon and apple aroma.

"You want whipped cream or vanilla ice cream?" I asked, poking my head into the fridge.

"After today, I think we need to indulge. So, both please," replied Sam.

"Agreed!" I added.

Ms. Pike pulled up a stool on the island and watched us youngsters finish making our dessert creations. She waited until we each found a stool around her before her questions began.

"So, the last time I saw you two was in the foyer where you left me standing there alone. Don't get me wrong, I am grateful that it led to finding Ellie, but I have to ask, how did you know where she was?" asked Ms. Pike.

I glanced over at Sam and waited for him to lead the conversation.

"Well," began Sam as he scooped a piece of pie into his mouth, "I guess it all started back in the forest when we were in search of the wolf that bit me," he said managing to swallow and then speak.

"Dearie, there is nothing that will surprise me, so just get to the point of the story," said Ms. Pike.

I laughed and decided to summarize for Ms. Pike, "The wolf that bit Sam ended up being cursed. Human by day and animal by night. So, Sam now has the same curse," I said.

"This curse has given me strange abilities. These abilities allowed me to track Ellie when no ordinary person could. This is what I am learning anyway," said Sam.

"And what are some of these abilities?" asked Ms. Pike.

"I can smell and hear things from a distance. Even the faintest of things I can pick up. I could smell the gas coming from Ellie's car and the blood from her wounds," Sam added.

"Now that makes sense," I said, finally understanding Sam's recent actions.

"I was even able to track you, Emily, in the forest by catching a scent of your hair in the wind," said Sam.

"Oh, you mean when you came to rescue me and I ended up rescuing you," I said laughing.

"I vaguely remember it happening that way," said Sam with a smirk.

"Well, nonetheless, that is definitely something new for this household. This makes you two quite a pair," said Ms. Pike with a slight wink.

"Why do you say that?" asked Sam.

"From what I can see, you both are experiencing a new world. And in this world, you are both learning and developing your new skills at the same time. Sam, with your heightened senses, and you, Emily, with your magic," stated Ms. Pike.

"She makes a good point," I added.

"A sorceress and a wolf, huh? That does make for an interesting pair," added Sam, scooping more pie into his mouth.

While we ate, we also filled Ms. Pike in on what Cy was working on in his lab for me.

"That is very intriguing, I must say. I may not understand all of Cy's techie goings-on, but I can and do appreciate his genius," said Ms. Pike.

Sam was nearly finished his second bowl while I had just finished off still my first when we heard Cy's voice echo through the house's intercom. We were being asked to return to the lab. Sam scooped up his last bite, and we both headed toward the elevators. Ms. Pike gladly cleaned up our dishes and cheerfully wished us good luck.

By the time we arrived at the lab, Cy had everything set up around the brain table. There was a chair hooked up with wires and a device that looked like a tablet mounted on a stand, facing the chair. Lying on the brain table all three visors rested with wires that connected onto the table as well.

"This looks very intricate, Cy," I said.

"The world of digital magic will with soon meet the world of mystical magic, if all goes well," concluded Cy.

"Very cool," added Sam.

"Where's Daniel?" asked Cy.

"He said he was going to the library," said Sam.

"He should be here very soon," I added.

"Okay then, let's get you set up, Emily," said Cy, motioning me to toward the chair.

While on the chair, Cy hooked up wires to my temples that seemed to connect to the brain table. The chair seemed to be the only piece of equipment not being connected to the brain table.

"Okay, Emily, this setup is designed to not only allow us to see and hear Serena when you communicate with her but also feel what she and you feel when you connect with each other," said Cy.

"What do you mean by feel? I never experienced Serena's feelings. I only usually hear her," I asked.

"Since Serena is within you, she should be able to send you images from her past—in other words, memories. And with each memory, there is usually a link to some emotion to help understand the image," said my father, joining the group around the brain table.

"Correct! And if she has not done that with you, try doing it now that you have an audience," said Cy.

"Oh, I get it," I said, nodding in agreement.

"Great. Now if you, Daniel, and you, Sam, can slip on the VR visors like so," said Cy, demonstrating how to put on the devices. "When we begin, remember, during this whole experience, we are only but spectators rather than participants. Serena will not be able to hear us or see us. So, it is important that we remain silent and let Emily do all the communicating," concluded Cy.

Once everyone was all geared up, Cy turned to me. "Okay, Emily, you are up. Use the tablet as you would your phone," he said.

I tapped on the tablet's screen and swiped to find the camera app. When the camera function popped up on the tablet's screen and I could see my own digital reflection, I began to call out Serena's name. When Serena's face came into view on the tablet screen, it was also captured on the brain table as well—however, in a three-dimensional image.

Sam, Daniel, and Cy were able to see the 3D image being projected above the brain table through their visors. Out of sheer curiosity, Sam lifted his visor from his face and looked toward the brain table. He saw nothing but the table. When he returned the visor to its resting place on his face, Serena's image reappeared.

"Whoa, this is cool," whispered Sam, amazed at what he was seeing.

Daniel and Cy took a more conservative reaction to seeing Serena and remained quiet.

"Emily, are you ready to learn more about your destiny?" said Serena.

"Absolutely! But first, I want you to know there are others who I trust that can see and hear you right now. I needed these people to know the urgency of your message. I hope you don't mind," I said respectfully.

"I appreciate you telling me that. And I welcome the audience," said Serena with a smile.

"Perfect. Also, if there is any way for us to connect on a different level say more visual, we can do it now," I said.

"I see, and yes, we can. So let's begin at the beginning," said Serena as her image blurred and the image of a fortress high above the clouds came into view.

"This is the exact fortress from my dreams. Is this my memory or yours?" I said in awe.

"This is my memory that was shared with you. This was the fortress of Avalon. It was a place of magic and magnificence. Within these walls housed a vault. This vault was made out of stone and marble," said Serena as the she changed the view to show the vault to me for the first time.

The vault's floor was made of white-colored stone while its walls were painted in white and gold marble. It was grand and elaborate as any exquisite museum would be. But instead of laser beams and alarm systems for protection as would be of today, this vault was protected by magic. This was evident by simply how the artifacts were displayed. Artifacts were not housed in solid cases or glass boxes. They merely just floated midair, above a stone or marble base. Some had a slight glow to them while others just hovered in a suspended state.

As I looked around the vault and closely at the floating artifacts, I noticed I had seen some of them before. There was a book levitating above a gold base and a medallion floating beside it. It was three years ago when I first saw these items; they were the book of Mystics and the medallion of Oris. When I glanced over to the corner of the vault, a vivid picture of a green gem suspended over a stone base came into view. And then just to the left of it was a gold staff that looked like a giant sewing needle about the length of one's arm. In the middle of the needle's eye rested a ruby-red gem. From these images, I had this sense of reverence and power. I could see there were other items, but strangely, only those artifacts come into view for me.

"Emily, what you see or have been shown are the only artifacts left from the vault. The rest were destroyed, as was the vault," said Serena, now showing me the image of the vault in ruins.

The walls were black with no luster and the stone floor cracked as if hit by an earthquake. There was a sense of loss and destruction in this image.

"This is horrible. Who would do something like this to such a place of beauty and wonder?" I asked.

"Only one person is to blame for this destruction. She schemed with other dark and evil sorcerers and sorceresses to break into the fortress and destroy the vault. The battle to defeat them was won in the end, however, at such a great cost. I lost my older sister and other guardians during this time," said Serena as her face returned to the screen.

"I'm sorry to hear about your sister. You talked about other guardians, who were they?" I asked.

"The alliance that formed the guardians of Avalon were made up of my sisters and I, the sorcerers of light, courageous noble kings, and the warrior elves. It was a bond of respect sealed by an oath to protect the weak and innocent. We all knew the value and importance of the artifacts as well as the danger of their power if used by evil," said Serena.

"Is the person who destroyed the vault connected to the evil force you warned me about?" I asked.

"Yes, it is actually one and the same. Her name is Zara. She calls herself the mistress of the dark," said Serena as her face faded and the face of another woman filled my screen.

A woman with bony cheeks and dark hair with purple streaks on the side of each came into view.

"Zara had the gift to shape-shift into any animal. She could transform at will into anything, but the larger the animal, the more of her power was used," said Serena as she showed another the image of Zara.

I saw Zara shifting into a black panther then to a slithery black boa constrictor. With each transformation, I noticed there was always a distinctive purple streak somewhere on the animal's body.

"Zara learned later that the animal she enjoyed the most shifting into was a bird: a big black bird," said Serena as her face returned to the screen.

"Why a bird?" I asked.

"A bird could go unnoticed, a bird could appear less threatening, and this is how the manipulation would begin," said Serena.

"How did you end up defeating her?" I asked.

"In the beginning, it was difficult because she had stolen the Jade Crystal from the vault. The power of the Jade Crystal made Zara unstoppable. It took many lives to retrieve the crystal from her and a few more to trap her in the bottle that became her prison for centuries," said Serena, showing a picture of an indigo-blue bottle being locked in a wooden box.

Beneath the visor, Sam gave out a short gasp. He had seen those items before.

Serena's face returned to the screen with a look of concern. "Emily, you have to understand that if Zara is released from the bottle, she will be after the Jade Crystal again," said Serena.

"Why is the crystal so important to her?" I asked.

"Well, not only does the crystal hold powerful magic any sorceress would desire, but for Zara, it protects her from her weakness. As powerful as Zara is, she grows weak every time she uses powerful magic. With the crystal, she will have an unlimited power source. She will stop at nothing to have it," warned Serena.

"I understand. What does the crystal do?" I asked.

"Like the book of Mystics and the medallion of Oris, each artifact processes a distinct power. The Jade Crystal could enhance its user's power by ten times. For instance, if someone had the gift of strength, with the crystal, they could move a mountain," said Serena.

"And, if someone had magic and processed the crystal…" I added.

"Well, I think you can image the danger that would cause," said Serena.

"What about the stick that looks like a giant sewing needle with the red ruby on it, what does that do?" I asked.

"That's the Phoenix Staff. It has the power to transport people to different places. It's the key to opening portals," said Serena.

"How does it work?" I asked.

"Let me show you," said Serena as an image of the staff being used manifested.

We watched as one of Serena's sisters created a ring of fire with the staff. Within that ring was a window to another place. As the ring grew larger, Serena's sister disappeared through it.

"How does the staff know what destination is intended?" I asked.

"The one who commands the staff need only think of a place and then form the ring of fire. A portal will be created to send anyone entering the ring to the intended destination," said Serena.

"Does Zara know where the Jade Crystal is? I remember you saying that it was only you that did," I said.

"In order to find the crystal, she will first look for me. Yet she does not know the physical me can no longer be found. This is our only advantage," said Serena.

"And the other artifacts, do you know where they all are?" I asked.

"Yes, I do. And your starting point will be the Jade Crystal. The other items will reveal itself once you find the Jade Crystal," said Serena.

"So, where is the crystal hidden?" I asked.

"I will show you," said Serena fading from the screen.

In her place, the screen showed the image of the green crystal embedded in a rock formation beneath some water. The more the image zoomed out to reveal the gem's true surroundings, the more familiar the hiding place felt to me. When Serena was able to show me the hiding place in full view, I knew why it felt so familiar.

Serena's face returned to the screen.

"Emily, you must find and retrieve the crystal. Since you have my power, the crystal and all the artifacts will call out to you. And lastly, you must remember that only those with immortal gifts can wield the power of each artifact," said Serena.

"Thank you, Serena, I promise I will do what you ask," I said with conviction.

"Good luck, Emily. I will always be here if you need me," said Serena fading from the screen.

As I watched Serena's face disappear, I saw Cy, my father, and Sam also remove their visors. Then Cy moved to my aid to detach me from my wires.

"Is it me, or was that the wildest thing someone could ever experience?" said Sam with enthusiasm.

"Well, it was certainly different," said Cy.

"Serena gave us a lot of information we can now move forward with," said my father.

"What do you think is our first move?" asked Cy to my father.

"Well, it seems pretty clear that we start with Emily finding the Jade Crystal," said my father.

"I agree," said Cy as he worked to free me from the wires.

"I think there is something I need to mention," interjected Sam.

"What is it, Sam?" asked my father.

"I recognized two items from Serena's images," said Sam.

"Which ones?" I asked.

"The blue bottle and the wooden box," said Sam.

"You saw these items before? Where?" I asked further.

"The night I was attacked. I found the box in the woods and brought to my camp. And then I opened the box and saw the bottle," said Sam.

"That's right! You did mention that in your story," concluded Cy.

"So, then Serena was right. Zara is that close. We don't know if anyone has opened the bottle. Anyone could have released her," said Sam.

"No, not just anyone. My research into the mystic world has always proven that only that of magic or immortal gift could release a spell or break one," said my father.

"So only someone of magic or immortality could open the bottle?" asked Sam.

"Yes, precisely," added Cy. "Even if you, at that time, tried to open it, Sam, it would not open for you," said Cy.

"Then we truly don't know if the bottle has been opened?" I asked.

"Correct. We don't know this yet," Cy added.

"Wait, what did you mother say about what she saw today?" said my father looking for my response.

"She mentioned a black bird of some type," I said, recalling my mother's story.

"And how many black big birds have purple stripes along its body?" concluded my father.

"So, it is possible that Zara is free," said Sam.

"Which makes finding the Jade Crystal more urgent," I said.

"I agree with Emily. The crystal was embedded in a rock formation of some sort. Emily, do you know where that rock formation is?" asked my father.

"Sure do," I added with certainty.

"Where?" asked Sam.

"At the very place where you and I first met. My cove," I said with a smile.

Sam gave a slight smirk toward my direction. "Of course!"

"Tomorrow at first daylight, we head for the cove," said my father.

"Wait, Cy, look up the low and high tides times in the area," I said.

"Sure, but why do you want to me do that?" asked Cy as he picked up his wireless keyboard.

"The crystal is embedded in one of the rock formations that is within the small cave near my cove. The cave fills up with water during high tides. So, we only have the low-tide period as the window to find it," I said.

"Cy, when is low tide?" asked my father.

"I can do better than that," said Cy typing in some data. He placed the keyboard down on the table then waved his hand from the brain table into the air, projecting a three-dimensional image of the cove's topography over the table for all of us to see.

"Nice work! I can see the cove. And there is the cave," I said, pointing to the particular area.

"If we shift the view slightly, we will be able to see how visible the opening to the cave will be at low tide," said Cy, continuing to type in other commands on his keyboard.

The view slightly tilted, and from the new angle, we could all see the cave's opening like Cy mentioned.

"Just waiting for the computer to calculate and pinpoint the low tide periods," said Cy, completing his last set of commands. "And voila!" concluded Cy.

We watched as a series of numbers scrolled up and down the brain table's image of the cove and when it all stopped, the information needed presented itself.

"Looks like low tide tomorrow starts at 11:00 a.m. and ends at about 3:00 p.m.," said my father.

"Precisely," added Cy.

"Okay then, Emily, you will have four hours to get the crystal. We head out tomorrow," said my father.

"Daniel, I think it is best I stay behind so I can work on creating a protective casing for the artifacts. After hearing from Serena, I may have some ideas about creating our own vault," said Cy.

"Good idea, Cy. I agree. Sam and I will go with Emily then," said my father.

We all agreed with the plan. Sam looked at the time and noticed how late it was getting. Sam sought Cy's attention and both men agreed it would be time to set up for the containment. Just as Sam was getting settled into his new nightly abode and Cy finished punching in the last digit activating the shield, the intercom crackled. Ms. Pike's voice echoed throughout the lab, asking for my father to urgently come to my mother' room.

"Something is wrong with the baby. Please come upstairs now!" pleaded Ms. Pike.

Without hesitation, my father and I raced toward the elevator.

When my father and I arrived in my mother's room, we found Ms. Pike by my mother's bedside, holding a cloth on my mother's forehead.

"Daniel, Ellie's burning up. She keeps saying the baby feels wrong," said Ms. Pike.

"Did you call the doctor?" I asked.

"Yes, he is on his way," said Ms. Pike.

"Ellie, I'm here," said my father.

"Daniel. The baby. It's not moving," cried my mother.

"Stay calm. The doctor is on his way. Everything will be okay," said my father calmly.

"Mom, what do you need?" I asked, trying to stay as calm as my father. When my mother looked in my direction, I could see the worry in her eyes. "You are going to be fine, Mom. You are going to be fine," I said, hoping to ease her worry.

The sound of a car pulling into driveway and the slam of a car door signaled the doctor's arrival.

"What do we have here?" asked the doctor, pushing through the door to my mother's room.

"Doc, Ellie says there is something wrong with the baby," said my father.

"Hmmm," said the doctor, grabbing is stethoscope from his bag.

We moved from my mother's bedside, allowing the doctor access for his examination.

"Ellie, it's Dr. Elliot. Besides a huge spike in your temperature, tell me what else is going on?" asked the doctor, placing the stethoscope unto Ellie's belly.

"I feel so tired and weak. And I can't feel the baby," said my mother.

"Hmmm," said the doctor, reaching into his bag again and pulling out a small portable machine with wires and circular patches.

"What is that, Dr. Elliot?" I asked.

"It's a monitor that will record the baby's vitals," said the doctor, attaching the circular pads to my mother's belly. "We can determine if the baby is in distress or not," he added.

We watched as the monitor beeped while numbers and the symbol of a heart digitally appeared on its screen. Dr. Elliot examined the monitor's results intently, but his final expression left us uneasy.

"I think there are multiple things happening here. Ellie's fever indicates an infection. But something else is causing the baby's heartbeat to become faint," said the doctor with concern.

"What do you need doctor?" asked my father.

"I can treat the infection, but before I do, I will need to get the baby out of Ellie first," concluded the doctor.

"Should we call the paramedics?" I asked.

"Um, honestly, by the time they get here, the baby could be in more jeopardy. I don't want to risk that," said the doctor. "Daniel, I will need to perform the C-section here. I will need your permission to allow this and some supplies to perform the surgery. These supplies can be found at my office," he added.

"You have my permission to do whatever you need. And we also have medical lab here in the mansion. Just tell us what supplies you need," said my father.

"Okay," said the doctor as he wrote down the list of items on a nearby notepad. "This is the bare minimum of what we need for supplies," added the doctor, handing the paper to my father.

My father reviewed the list and confirmed we had what was needed in Cy's lab.

"I can assist you, Doctor. I used to be a midwife many moons ago," said Ms. Pike, still holding the cloth over Ellie's forehead.

The doctor nodded and began to prepare himself for what was needed next.

"What can I do?" I asked, feeling somewhat helpless.

"It is best you and your father stay outside during surgery. But what you can do right now is gather some warm towels and find all your clean linens and bring them here to the room," said the doctor with decisive urgency.

My father and I set out from the room and raced to fulfill our tasks. My father raced to the lab, and I ran to the linen closet to gather what I needed. After several minutes, I had gathered my items and brought them to the room. By then, my father had also arrived with the medical supplies needed.

"Doc, is there anything else we can do to help?" asked my father.

Before leading us out of the room, the doctor turned to the both of us. "I can assure you Ellie and the baby will be fine. I have done this procedure many times even in the worst of conditions. I used to be a field medic before going to my private practice. Everything will be fine," said the doctor, hoping to provide us with the assurance we needed.

My father nodded and agreed to finally allow the doctor to do what he needed to do by closing the door of the bedroom that now turned into a medical facility.

Standing in the hallway, I felt myself fall into my father's chest; and as I wrapped my arms around his waist, I began to feel my eyes swell up with tears. His arms wrapped around my shoulders.

"What is going on with Ellie?" asked Cy, coming up the hallway.

"It's the baby. The doctor has to do a C-section," said my father.

"I gathered surgery was necessary when I noticed you took some of medical instruments. But what happened? I thought Ellie and baby were fine," asked Cy.

"We don't know. Mom just started to have a fever, and the baby was in trouble," I said, wiping my cheeks.

"Maybe the car accident caused this, but the effects must have taken time to manifest," added my father.

"Who is Ellie's doctor?" asked Cy.

"Dr. Elliot," replied my father.

"Dr. David Elliot?" asked Cy.

"Yes, that is him," said father.

"Hmmm. David and I have crossed paths before during my military days. I can assure you he is very good. And in times of urgency, he comes highly recommended. I wouldn't worry, Ellie and the baby are in good hands," said Cy.

Cy's statement about Dr. Elliot provided some comfort, but being forced to wait outside the hallway left us all feeling equally helpless.

The countless minutes we all stood outside the door of my parents' bedroom just hoping to hear something about my mother turned into hours. Cy returned to the lab to keep watch over Sam and work on his new ideas on the vault while my father and I turned one of the rooms across the hall into a waiting room.

"Mom and the baby are going to be okay, right?" I asked, turning to my father.

"They are going to be just fine. Your mom is tougher than you think," said my father.

"You know, I thought my life was different after hearing from Serena, but it is really going to change once this baby comes," I said.

"You are so right, Emily. But I want you to remember that no matter what happens, you still need to follow your own path. The gift that was given to you is what it is, a gift. I don't think Serena would have given it to just anyone," said my father.

"I know. All these years you, Mom, and Cy have always been there for me, and it's hard to imagine not having you always there with me," I said.

"We will always be here for you, Emily. But you need to understand, sometimes, we can only go so far. Eventually, your journey will have to be taken on your own," said my father.

"You are referring to the artifacts, aren't you?" I asked.

"Yes. You need to find them. And you need to protect them. That is your new path. I need to stay here and protect my family, this is my responsibility," said my father.

"What if I am not strong enough? Serena talked about dark magic, and what do I do if I come up against it?" I asked.

"Emily, sometimes it's not about being stronger or more powerful, it's about being smarter. When I was in my library waiting for Cy to finish the virtual reality setup, I came across some very interesting finds. All ancient readings or stories from the mystic world have a common truth. We refer to them as universal truths," said my father.

"What are universal truths?" I asked curiously.

"Well, they are inevitable certainties, such as everything that goes up must come down, everything that has a beginning will have an end, and when there is darkness there is also light. Do you see where I am getting at?" said my father.

"I think so. Anything that is lost will eventually be found," I added.

"Exactly! You just need to be smart enough to discover what inevitable certainty will play out," said my father.

Just as I was about to make a comment to my father, loud beeping sounds came from my mother's room along with an even louder crashing sound. By the time we arrived at my mother's door, the beeping had stopped, leaving only silence in the room. My father and I looked at each other. In that moment, we were afraid of what that silence meant; we were afraid of what was waiting for us behind this door. As I placed my hand on the doorframe and leaned my forehead onto the door, a sudden sweet sound of a baby crying and the unlocking of the doorknob replaced our fear with joy. When the door finally opened after hours of waiting, my father and I walked into the room to find my mother smiling, holding my new baby sister.

Chapter

19

The evening sky back at Rick's cabin was calm with only a few stars out to blanket the night. Rick had already transformed and walked onto the porch where Zara sat on the chair. The rest of the pack were slowly awakening from their slumber and lifting themselves to all fours, awaiting Zara's next command. Zara stood up from the chair and walked to the front of the porch so she could be in clear view for the pack.

"Rise, my soldiers, and come meet your new pack leader," said Zara out loud.

The pack moved as one toward Zara. When they approached the porch, Rick, in wolf form, walked up front and stood alongside Zara.

"This is Rick," said Zara, but this time, the words were not spoken out loud but in the minds of each member of the pack.

The pack all looked up toward Rick and bowed their heads. Rick looked down at the pack and then back up at Zara. It was time for Rick to embrace his leadership role and the power it will wield from this point on. Rick moved toward the edge of the porch and tested his authority.

"We will hunt tonight. We search for someone who is to join our pack," said Rick with words not spoken out loud but in the minds of each member of the pack.

Each member of the pack howled back toward Rick. And within their howling reply, Rick could hear their thoughts and knew they heard him. Each member of the pack understood his command. As

Rick walked down the porch steps, the pack stepped back from their spot, allowing Rick to move past them, like a lion king passing through his pride.

Zara, now in full magical strength, crouched to the floor and shape-shifted into a big black bird. Now as a bird she spoke to Rick telepathically, *"I will lead from above while you lead from below."*

Rick nodded and replied, *"Fly north. His scent is strong in that direction."*

Zara lifted her wings and began to soar into the night sky in the direction Rick mentioned. Once the big black bird left to begin the search, Rick led his pack into the woods. The pack raced behind Rick at a pace faster than any human could. Rick and the pack maneuvered through trees with stealth-like dexterity and weaved between the bushes and trails with ease. What would have taken a couple hours by car to arrive at their destination, Rick and the pack were able to reduce that time frame down to more than half because they did not have to follow any paved road. They created their own path toward Sam's scent. A scent that took them directly to the mansion. Outside the mansion and perched upon a branch next to a certain bedroom window was Zara. From the branch, Zara could see all that was happening in that room. And watched she did, very intently, recalling her encounter with the woman and the car. When the pack and Rick finally arrived, they emerged from the darkness of the trees and began moving up to the driveway. Rick ordered his pack to circle the building while he communicated with Zara.

"What is your next command, mistress?" asked Rick telepathically.

"We wait until opportunity. But first, I need to reach who we are here for," replied Zara.

Rick nodded and ordered his pack to guard the perimeter of the mansion. The pack did as commanded and were soon camouflaged by the darkness.

Zara attempted to connect with Sam telepathically.

Back in the lab and still unaware of the news of the new baby, Cy focused all his attention on the vault casing and design. Sam's transformation went smooth, and the containment room performed to par. Occasionally, Cy checked on Sam. As Cy was nearing Sam's room, Sam let out a loud howl. When Cy reached the invisible door to the room, he saw Sam shaking his head and pacing frantically across the floor. *What is wrong with Sam,* thought Cy.

—⟶⟵—

Zara was now linked to Sam. She could hear his thoughts, and he could hear hers.

"*Who are you?*" said Sam, trying to figure out the voice he was hearing in his head.

"*I am Zara,*" replied Zara.

"*Zara! How? What do you want with me?*" gasped Sam.

"*I wish you to join my army. You, like Rick, are special. I wish to have you both,*" said Zara.

"*Rick?! You can't have me. I am locked up. I am keeping everyone safe,*" said Sam.

"*Dear boy, no one is safe from me. Freedom will be yours soon,*" said Zara.

Sam's human eyes looked at Cy standing outside his shield. Sam wanted to warn Cy of the danger that was close, but his wolf form didn't allow him to. Sam was beginning to realize that in wolf form, Zara had a hold over him. Suddenly, Cy's phone began to beep, giving off perimeter breach alerts.

—⟶⟵—

Outside the mansion, Zara seized the opportunity and gave Rick the command for the pack to attack, starting at the back entrance. Rick howled at the pack, giving the order. The entire pack began to ram the door with their bodies and sharp destructive claws. When Rick arrived at the back entrance, he ordered two members of the pack to break through the windows while he and the others continued to break down the door. The growling and the clawing at the windows soon proved successful as the glass from the frame shattered, allowing them a way into the house. The pack quickly moved through the broken window and found themselves inside the mansion. Rick moved to the head of the pack and looked around at the room they had entered. The room appeared to be more of a storage area, something a caretaker would access. Rick realized that although they had entered the mansion, they had not completely broken through to the interior, and they needed to find another way to accomplish this. One of the wolves from his pack howled, signaling a hint to a possible solution. Rick moved to the wolf's call and saw another way they could penetrate atop one of the walls in the room, but they would need Zara's help to achieve this.

Rick telepathically summoned Zara from her perch on the tree. Once Zara arrived at the storage room, Rick and the pack relayed the plan to gain access inside the mansion's interior. Rick and the pack began the first phase of the plan by tearing down shelves and maintenance equipment from the walls. The commotion was just a distraction. While half of the pack worked at destroying the room, the other half worked at prying free a vent cover on one of the walls. With the cover gone, Zara transformed into a small garner snake and went unnoticed, slithering her way into the vent shafts, finding an end that would lead her to one of the main rooms of the house. Once she arrived at her destination, the pack would then move to the outside of the house and wait for Zara to allow an opportunity to enter. Zara slithered her way down the shaft, twisting a turning around corners, dragging her long body. Finally, she came to one end of the shaft that led into what appeared to be a living room area. The holes from this vent were bigger than that from the storage room's, so Zara was able to slither through the vent's grade with ease and onto the room's carpet. Once she was clear from the vent and in the middle of the room, she transformed into her human form and opened the window, giving her pack access. The pack, by then, had left the storage room and were outside, looking for Zara's opportunity. Upon seeing the open window, the pack quickly jumped through the windowpane and one by one landed in the living room. When all the pack members were now inside the room and moved toward the opened doorway, silent motion indicators went off, causing larger vertical steel doors to close. As the doorways were closing, Zara used her magic to slide a large table into the doorway, suddenly stopping the steel door from reaching the floor and giving way to the wolves to crawl beneath the table and move into the hallway. Zara quickly changed back into a bird and flew beneath the table behind the wolves just as the steel door lowered and crushed the table wedged between the frame. Zara and the pack quickly maneuvered through the hallway and focused on finding what they came there to retrieve.

Cy left Sam's area and ran to the monitors to identify the breach. He saw the wolves destroy the storage room and then, for some reason, leave the storage room to then suddenly reappear in the living room. And after watching the table get crushed under the door, Cy began to feel somewhat concerned.

Frantically sending commands into his keyboard, Cy tried to contain the animals that were now inside the mansion. But they were moving too fast, and the security doors were too slow. The wolves were escaping past them. Cy's main concern was the safety of everyone on the upper levels.

Cy turned toward the intercom, "Daniel! We have intruders. Keep everyone upstairs. I am initiating upper-level defense systems," commanded Cy.

"Cy, wait! Who caused the breach?" asked Daniel from the intercom.

"Wolves, Daniel! We have wolves in the mansion!" replied Cy.

—◦◦◦—

The news of the threat to our home struck everyone in my parents' room with concern.

"Did he say wolves?" I asked my father.

"Yes, he did," said my father.

"Emily, I need you to stay here with everyone. I need to get to Cy before the defense systems are initiated. You will all be safe here," said my father as he quickly bent down to kiss my mother's forehead and my new baby sister's little head.

"Daniel, wait, I will go with you. You will need someone to cover your back," said Dr. Elliot.

I watched my father agree to Dr. Elliot's help. Then both men ran out of the room minutes before the defense system was initiated, leaving behind myself, Ms. Pike, and my mother alone in the room.

"What are wolves doing in our home?" asked Ms. Pike.

"I wish I knew," said my mother, trying to keep the baby from crying.

There has to be a reason, I thought.

Just then, I heard Serena call out my name. I left Ms. Pike and my mother in the room and walked into the bathroom and closed the door.

Staring at the bathroom mirror, I called out for Serena; and within seconds, Serena's face appeared.

"Emily, there is a reason why they are here," said Serena.

"You mean the wolves?" I asked.

"Yes, these wolves are not alone. They have help. Zara is here. She is leading the wolves," said Serena with urgency.

"Why? Does she think the artifacts are here?" I asked.

"That's not why she is here. She wants something else—or better still, someone else," said Serena.

"What does she want? Who does he want?" I asked.

"She wants Sam," said Serena.

"Sam? Why Sam?" I questioned.

"That part I don't know. She could be building her own army—" said Serena

"An army of wolves," I stated.

"It is possible," said Serena.

"You mean wolves like Rick and Sam, cursed wolves?" I asked.

"No, Rick and Sam are of a different, breed and she knows this by now. Their curse has magic, and she will use it to destroy everything and everyone in her path to get what she wants," said Serena.

"And she wants the crystal, right?" I added.

"Yes, and more. If the crystal falls to her, she will use it to gain power and dominion over everyone," Serena said with concern.

"How can the curse that Rick and Sam share help Zara?" I asked.

"Since their curse was once created by magic, she can create a telepathic link to them while they are in animal form. This link can make them do things she wants them to do, even allow her to see what they have seen or know what they know, almost as if they were under a mind-control spell," said Serena.

"Zara can't get to Sam!" I gasped. "Sam knows where the Jade Crystal is," I said.

"Emily, you must stop Zara from getting Sam or get to the Jade Crystal before Sam tells Zara where it is hidden," Serena pleaded.

I thanked Serena for her help and watched her disappear from the mirror as I ran out of the bathroom toward the intercom.

"Cy, it's Emily. The wolves are here for Sam. Don't let them take Sam!" I yelled.

Still inside the mansion, Rick and the other wolves worked at ramming the elevator doors. Driving their huge claws into the middle the metal doors, they pulled each door apart, creating an opening big enough for them to jump into. As they descended, they leaped from one elevator shaft wall to the next, scratching their claws before reaching the lower floor leading to the lab.

"They're already here, Emily," replied Cy through the intercom.

Cy scrambled around his lab in search for some type of a way defend himself. Grabbing hold of a long tube, Cy waited anxiously for the wolves to break through the elevator doors leading to the lab. The pounding at the doors and the crushing sound of metal echoed outside the lab. Sam couldn't contain his animal nature. He ran his crawls against the walls of his containment room and attempted to throw his body into the shield door, which only resulted in him being deflected and landing on the floor.

I need to help Cy, Sam thought as his human side tried desperately to fight against the animal rage.

The wolves finally broke through the elevator doors and ran into the lab. Just as one crossed the lab's opening threshold, Cy launched the contents from his canon tube. A ball-like figure shot from the canon and hurled toward one of the wolves. As it made contact, the ball opened to a net, catching one of the wolves and stopping them in their tracks. He had trapped one animal, but more were making their way in toward

Sam's containment room. Cy fired another shot, but it missed. Cy knew that the only thing that stood between the wolves and Sam was him, and he was not willingly going to give up the code to Sam's containment door. Cy now found himself trapped in a corner of his lab by three of the wolves. When the fourth wolf arrived, Cy noticed it was bigger than the others. It walked up behind the wolves slowly and just towered over them from behind.

"You are not going to get him. I can guarantee that," shouted Cy as he noticed a big black bird fly into the lab and land behind the large wolf.

Cy watched as the bird disappeared behind the animal and then suddenly change into something else. What finally came to be was a woman dressed in black. Cy recognized her instantly from Serena's images.

"Zara, I presume," said Cy sarcastically.

"Yes, I am she," said Zara smiling.

"What do you want with Sam?" asked Cy.

"What I want does not concern you. What I need from you does. Open the door," said Zara with a look of authority.

"No, so you can take your wolf pack and go," said Cy.

"Hahaha," laughed Zara. "You don't know what I can do. Let me show you," said Zara as she began to rub her hand palms together and chant.

Creeping up behind the large wolf, she thrust her palm into the wolf's back. The wolf yelped and then crouched to the floor. Within seconds, Cy witness the animal change; it changed into a man. The man was Rick, who quickly grabbed a lab coat nearby and covered himself as he attempted to stand on his two legs.

"Rick? How is this possible?" asked Cy, bewildered.

"Cy, we only came here for Sam. Please just give Zara what she wants, and no one will get hurt," said Rick.

"I won't," said Cy.

Zara started to move toward Cy. The wolves slowly backed up, giving her way toward Cy.

"If you won't give me what I want, then I will take it," said Zara, reaching out her hand and hovering over Cy's head.

"Cy, you have no clue what she is capable of, just tell her the code to the door," warned Rick.

"No!" said Cy sternly.

"So be it," said Zara as she started to chant while hovering her hand over Cy's head.

Cy began to yell, falling to the ground, holding his head. Zara continued to chant louder. Cy was now screaming in pain, feeling as though his head was about to explode. He could feel her in it, pulling and poking at his brain with what felt like electrical probes. Zara stopped chanting but still held her hand over Cy's head.

"Ahh, there is it, I have it. The code is 19722210. Rick, unlock the door," said Zara. "We are not finished. You have more use to me," added Zara, staring down at Cy.

Rick quickly left Zara and hurried over to Sam's containment room and punched in the code. The invisible shield released, and without warning, Sam ran out of the containment room.

Kneeling on the floor, Cy looked up at Zara. "Now you will be part of my army," said Zara, rubbing her hands together and chanting more magical words.

Zara bent down, and just as she was about to thrust her palm into Cy's chest, Sam leaped on top of her, forcing her to the floor away from Cy. Rick came running from behind Sam and shouted for Sam to stop, but Sam's animal rage stood before them and Cy.

Zara lifted herself to her feet and stared at Sam, who appeared to be protecting Cy.

"You have humanity in you," said Zara out loud.

Sam stood his ground and just growled, trying to block Zara from entering his head.

"But I have power," said Zara telepathically to Sam.

"Get out of my head," said Sam.

"Do you think you can protect them? I can make you destroy them if I want to," cackled Zara, beginning her control over Sam.

Sam began to feel the magical link Zara was forcing upon him. He tried to break the connection by shaking his head, but the link was too strong. Sam soon fell into a succumbing state. His growling subsided, and his stance changed from defiance to submissiveness.

"You see what I can do," said Zara.

Sam could feel his control fade, and Zara's voice became the only thought in his mind. Cy watched as Sam turned from protector to becoming a member of Zara's pack. Just as Sam was almost completely under Zara's spell, the intercom crackled, and the voice on the other end became the only voice Sam heard in that moment.

"Cy, it's Emily. Is Sam okay? Sam can you hear me? It's Emily," Emily said, not realizing how her voice echoed throughout the lab.

Cy watched as the sound of Emily's voice somehow resonated with Sam, breaking Zara's link for a moment. Cy raced to the intercom and replied to Emily so her voice would continue throughout the lab.

"Cy, my father and Dr. Elliot are on their way to you," Emily continued, unaware of what was happening in the lab.

Sam continued to struggle, hoping to break from Zara's link permanently, but Zara reinforced her control and sent another strong magical link, breaking whatever last attempt Sam had to be free. Cy scrambled once again to make another reply to Emily, but the other wolves ceased his attempt by quickly pushing some lab equipment toward him. A hurled table connected with Cy's head, sending him to the floor.

"Sam, just come with us now. That is all she wants," pleaded Rick.

"There is more to lose by staying here," said Zara to Sam.

"What do you mean?" Sam asked.

"If you stay, I will be forced to hurt everyone here, even the baby," said Zara.

Sam soon realized that Zara was referring to Ellie's unborn child.

Emily made one last attempt on the intercom to communicate with Cy.

"Cy are you there? Sam!" Emily shouted, and as her voice echoed throughout the lab, so did the sound of her new baby sister's cry.

Sam now knew Ellie had given birth and understood the danger he was placing all of them.

"Your humanity will not allow you to risk their lives, true?" said Zara.

Defeated, Sam agreed to leave with the pack under the condition that no one is to be hurt. They would leave the mansion through the fire escape back stairwell, avoiding any contact with anyone.

"Your terms are accepted," said Zara walking over to Rick and magically transformed him back into a wolf while then shape-shifting into her bird form.

The entire pack, led by Rick, all exited the lab through the back stairwell with Zara flying ahead, leaving behind an unconscious Cy lying on the floor of the lab.

Chapter

20

By the time Daniel and Dr. Elliot arrived in the lab, the intruders were gone. Dr. Elliot raced to the unconscious Cy while Daniel disengaged the defense systems on the upper levels.

"How is he, Doc?" asked Daniel.

The doctor quickly examined Cy. "I think he just got knocked out," said the doctor, pulling a small pill-like object from his pocket.

The doctor broke the pill and lifted it to Cy's nose. Cy subconsciously inhaled the scent and was soon waking up from his unconscious state. Shaking his head, Cy tried to regain his memory of the events.

"Sam...," said Cy with a cough. They have Sam," added Cy, slowly gaining consciousness.

"Who?" asked Daniel.

Dr. Elliot was able to get Cy to a chair to examine him further while Daniel continued to find out what happened.

"Wolves, Rick, and Zara came here for Sam," said Cy.

"Why?" asked Daniel.

"I don't know. But I do know all they wanted was him," said Cy in between deep breaths as Dr. Elliot examined Cy's chest for further injuries.

"I think I know why," Emily said, entering the lab.

"Emily! How's your mother and the baby?" asked Daniel.

"Everyone is fine. The defense systems kept everyone safe upstairs. But it also kept me from coming down here, until now," she said.

Once Dr. Elliot finished his examination on Cy and concluded he was fine, he asked to check on Ellie and the baby one last time before leaving.

"Thank you, Doctor, for everything today. We are so sorry we put you through such an odd day," said my father.

"Think nothing of it. The chaos and urgency of today reminded me of my army medic days. I'm just glad I was here to help. Sounds like you all have more of a challenge ahead of you. If there is anything you need, or if I can help you all in any way, just let me know," said Dr. Elliot, shaking Daniel's hand and patting Cy's shoulder. "Just like the good ole days, right, Cy?" the doctor added with a chuckle.

"Copy that," said Cy with a salute.

—⬩—

Cy then turned to me to continue his inquiry. "So, why do you think they wanted Sam?" asked Cy.

"It's because of the curse both Rick and Sam share. Zara can use the magic within that curse to control them when they are in animal form," I said.

"No wonder Sam looked and acted so odd," stated Cy. "I mean one minute he is protecting me, and then he seemed confused," said Cy.

"It must have been Zara's control," said my father, "I did some research and found some evidence of this curse. There is a definite mystical link to it. If magic is the cause of the link, then only magic will be able to control it or maybe even change it."

"That could explain how Zara was able to force a transformation with Rick," said Cy pensively.

"What do you mean force a transformation?" I asked.

"She changed him from wolf to human right here before me," said Cy.

"Interesting," added my father.

"So, let me get this straight, Zara was able to transform Rick from wolf to human at will. And she can communicate with animals, therefore command them to do her will. How did she get Sam out of the containment room?" I asked.

"She was able to somehow get into my head and extract the code, very painfully I might add," said Cy.

"I am assuming she used magic again," I said.

"Must have and then was going to use it again to do something else to me, but before she could finish, Sam came to my rescue," said Cy.

"Sam?" asked my father.

"Yes, remember I said he was protecting me. Sam came to my defense while in wolf form," said Cy.

"See, I told you, Father, even though Sam is in wolf form, his human side is still very present. I saw it and felt it when we first encountered his change," I said.

"Emily is right. I saw how Zara's power was trying to control Sam, but I also saw a small glimmer of hope that helped Sam try and break free from that," said Cy.

"What did you see?" asked my father.

"Well, it was more of what Sam heard that helped him. He heard your voice, Emily, over the intercom. Your voice somehow helped him resist Zara for a brief time," said Cy.

"My voice? Me?" I questioned, until I remembered what Serena told me.

"Okay, so let's sort this out. We know Zara's magic is strong. We know she can control animals, specifically Rick and Sam. What we don't know is what her plans are," said my father.

"Based on what Serena has told us about Zara, she is a conqueror. Now that she is out of her prison, she will want to conquer this new world. And any military strategist knows that to win any battle, you need to be the most powerful and you need an army," said Cy.

"Which means she will be after the Jade Crystal more than ever now," said my father.

"Precisely," said Cy.

"Then it will be a race as to who will get to it first," I said.

"We are the only ones who know where it is, how can it be a race?" questioned my father.

"Sam is part of that *we*. Once Zara gets into Sam's head, she will know what we know," I concluded.

A look of concern flooded my father's and Cy's faces once they realized the severity of the situation.

"Looks like our plan is pretty clear," said my father.

"Yes, we find and retrieve the Jade Crystal and we get Sam back," added Cy.

"What about Zara and her army of wolves? How do we go about defeating them?" I asked.

"Well, we have to find out what their weaknesses are and use it," said Cy.

All that my father and Cy were strategizing made sense, and I would agree to it all. Yet as we planned to face this next challenge together, I feared that there would be that one moment I would have to ultimately face personally. Before I confront Zara, any doubt, any disbelief in myself would have to be laid to rest. Stepping out of my cocoon, I must become who that I am and who Serena sees me to be. And lastly, to save Sam, my heart pleads that I won't have to make good on my promise to him.

—⁜—

Very late in that evening, the pack arrived at Rick's cabin, with Sam amongst them. Zara shape-shifted back into human form and commanded the rest of the pack to stand guard around the cabin while she conversed with Rick and Sam inside the cabin. Zara decided to keep both Rick and Sam in wolf form to maintain her mental control over them. Both animals followed Zara into the cabin. Zara found the closest chair and sat down, looking to gain some needed rest from tonight's events. As she sat on the chair, Rick lay down on the floor while Sam just continued to stand on all fours, still trying to hold on to his identity.

"You still persist on fighting me," said Zara, getting comfortable on a wooden rocking chair.

"I am just trying to hold on to who I am," said Sam.

Zara laughed. *"Who you are is now dictated by me,"* she added.

Sam refused to believe that.

"What do you want from me?" asked Sam.

"I want you to be part of my army. It's simple," said Zara.

"What are your plans for this army of yours?" asked Sam.

Zara glanced over at Rick, who had been paying close attention to the conversation and then back over at Sam.

"Spread fear. Take what I want, and make sure no one gets in our way," answered Zara.

"What if I choose not to be part of all this?" asked Sam.

"I don't think you have choice in the matter," said Zara.

"I can refuse," said Sam with authority.

"If you refuse then like I said to you before, you have people you will lose. People I will hurt or people I will make you hurt for me," said Zara sternly.

Sam knew Zara was right. Just as he chose to protect his friends back at the mansion, Sam must also choose to protect them from Zara the best that he can. Yet if he had to choose between his life and his friends, he knew what choice that would be.

"Now that we have Sam, what is next?" asked Rick.

"We must find the whereabouts of the Jade Crystal. I need my powers to be at its peak. I cannot create my army until I have it!" said Zara with frustration.

Sam knew that the only way he could protect his friends would be to keep the crystal's whereabouts hidden from Zara at least for as long as he could. Emily needed time to find the crystal and keep it safe.

"Rick, take our new friend to your basement, and both of you await the dawn for your transformation. It's late, and I need time to rest," said Zara.

Rick obeyed and led Sam to the lower level where they would cage themselves until the nearing dawn arrived. As they descended, Sam had some questions for Rick.

"Why are you doing this? Why are you with her?" asked Sam.

"Zara can give me what I have always wanted," replied Rick.

"And what is that?" asked Sam.

"To be normal. To be human again and no longer cursed," said Rick.

"How do you know she can do that or even will do that for you?" asked Sam.

"Zara and I made a deal. I help her, and she helps me. It's that simple. She just needs this crystal to do it," said Rick, nearing the end of the staircase.

Sam started to wonder what price he would pay to not be cursed. Sam also began to understand Rick's motivation.

"*Tell me more about what this crystal will help Zara accomplish?*" asked Sam.

"*For starters, she can make more wolves like the ones outside. She says the wolves outside are like us—they were once human. But since she created them, they cannot change like us, unless she wills it,*" said Rick.

"*Those wolves are humans forced to be animals!*" said Sam.

"*Yes. I have seen how powerful her magic is. So, I wouldn't keep pushing back at her, if you know what is good for you,*" said Rick.

"*Well, she is not the only one with magic,*" mumbled Sam under his breath.

"*What did you say?*" asked Rick overhearing part of Sam's remark.

"*Nothing,*" replied Sam, quickly attempting to pull off an innocent look.

Rick looked back at Sam and glared. Rick allowed Sam to walk into cage first and then closed the door behind him.

"*You ask a lot of questions, boy! My gut tells me you know more than you are telling me. Zara will get it out of you. All it takes is one touch from her,*" warned Rick as he stood guard outside the cage door, ensuring Sam would not escape.

Behind the bars of the cell, Sam wished he could take back what he said. Now that Rick had his suspicions, he was not going to let them go so easily. Sam knew firsthand what it felt like to be under Rick's eye, giving him more concern than ever; his remark may have put his friends and especially Emily in danger.

Chapter

21

My night was restless. But what was more daunting was the thought of Sam held captive by Zara. I was still so new to this magical world that I wondered if what I knew was going to be enough to save Sam or, more still, face Zara. When I finally managed to fall asleep, I was allowed a glimpse into another page of my destiny.

I was back within the golden marble walls of Avalon's Vault. I felt the image so vividly, almost as if I were there. When I glanced around, I saw Serena standing alongside another woman whom I could not recognize. Both women walked about the vault together and then stopped at the Jade Crystal as it magically floated above its base. I felt as though I was eavesdropping on their conversation yet at the same time somehow given permission. The exchange between the two women was warm, compassionate, and familiar, almost family-like. It was soon that I realized she was one of Serena's sisters. The way the woman looked at Serena led me to think she was the eldest one. The two women stood around the artifact and joined hands, creating a circle around the crystal. They began chanting. The words were foreign to me at first, and then suddenly, the tongue changed to English and I could understand what they were saying.

"Power at be, bind to thee," said the two women over and over.

The handheld circle they created around the crystal soon created a wind tunnel between them that hovered above the gem. Serena looked up at the mini cyclonic swirl and stopped chanting; the older sister did not stop. Instead, she began a new chant with words I could not understand. As the older sister spoke louder and louder, the swirl of wind moved above Serena and slowly started to lower down, engulfing her and the crystal. The older sister watched as Serena and the crystal were trapped in the swirling wind, causing their hands to break free from each other. Serena and the crystal were lifted above the vault's floor by the now-rising, swirling wind. Within the funnel, Serena's body stood catatonic while the glowing emerald green crystal circled around her.

"The bond is complete," said Serena's sister as she watched the swirling wind slowly die down, lowering Serena and the crystal back to their resting places.

Standing back on the ground, Serena looked up at her sister and asked, "Did it work?"

The older sister smiled and nodded. "You and the crystal are bound together for eternity," she concluded.

I watched as Serena held the crystal in her hands and then turned her head to the side, as if staring directly at me. "As it is bound to you too, Emily," said Serena.

I awoke abruptly to the sound of a baby crying. It was a sound I still couldn't get used to in this house but still urged me to rise from by bed nonetheless. Still unable to shake the feeling of awe from the dream, I made my way to check on my new baby sister we named Lilly.

The nursery was filled with fluffy pink and white pillows and blankets. As well as adorable stuffed animals alongside the shelves. A white rocking chair stood by a set of French doors that, when opened, led out onto a wooden balcony that overlooked the mermaid water fountain. Lilly's room was the ultimate baby room with the best view. As soon as I entered her room, the aroma of lavender and baby powder filled my senses. Lilly was lying in her bassinet, fussing. I noticed her blanket that worked to keep her tightly wrapped like a burrito had come undone.

"Looks like you fought your way out of this one," I said, referring to her blanketed cocoon.

I rewrapped the blanket all nice and tight. I lifted her out of the bassinet and made my way to the rocking chair to have some sisterly quality time. I rocked with Lilly for a few minutes, hoping to watch her fall back to sleep.

"I told you she would know what kind of sister you would be," said my mother, watching me from the door.

"She is so little. It's hard to believe I have a sister," I said, cradling the little bundle in my arms.

My mother walked into the room and stood by the chair. "I remember when you were that small. I remember it like it was yesterday," said my mother.

"I bet my coming into this world wasn't as adventurous as hers," I said.

"Actually, yes, it was," said my mother.

"What?" I asked.

"The day I gave birth to you was also the day I thought I was going to lose you for the first time," said my mother.

"I don't think you ever told me this story. All you ever said was that I was born in Arizona. I just assumed in a hospital," I said.

"Your actual birth was not in a hospital, and I didn't tell you this story because it didn't seem important until now," said my mother.

"Well, you have to tell me now," I said eagerly, willing to listen.

My mother laughed and continued, "I was completing one of my last expeditions in Arizona. I had planned to be back home and safe by the time you arrived. But you had other plans, and so did the Jeep I was riding in," said my mother.

"So, I wasn't born in a hospital?" I questioned.

"Not quite. I was driving back to the hotel with some colleagues, and because it was so hot during that time, everyone was dripping in sweat. I didn't even notice my water break until the seat and my pants became soaked. The driver panicked and started to speed up, hoping to get me to the closest hospital. I was sitting in the back, trying to remain calm, while my colleagues kept an eye on me. Being preoccupied with my condition, the driver didn't notice a large boulder in the road. The Jeep hit the boulder and swerved off road, almost colliding with a tree. The boulder damaged the wheel underneath the Jeep, so getting back on the road was not going to be possible. We were in the middle of nowhere with little cell phone reception, and you were coming. I was a bit banged up from the Jeep going off the road but was more concerned for you and how I was going to deliver you in these conditions. It was dirty. It was hot, and it was dusty. Not the most ideal place I wanted my firstborn to come into this world. But you were so determined to come, and I couldn't stop it,"

"What happened next?" I asked.

"The driver left the Jeep to find a decent cell reception to call an ambulance. While myself and my colleagues prepared to deliver you right then and there in the back seat. Luckily for me, one of my colleagues had a medical background. It seemed like hours before you finally came. I delivered you on that hot dusty day in that back seat just minutes before the ambulance had found us. I looked down at your little face and your little hands. And was in awe at how determined you were to be part of this world. You and your sister have the same fighting spirit," said my mother.

"Well, we come from very good fighting genes," I said with a smile.

"Maybe, and I think that is why I am always afraid for you, yet at that same time, I know your will to never give up. You persevere even in the hardest of situations. That is what makes you so strong. Don't forget that," said my mother, noticing I did a good job putting Lilly to sleep.

"You know, I sometimes forget that about myself. Especially now with everything changing and me forever being changed. I worry about how long I have with all of you," I said, lifting Lilly up to my mother to place back in her bassinet.

"Emily, you are becoming the person you are meant to be," said my mother, laying Lilly down in her bassinet. "And I know it is scary at times and maybe even different, but I truly believe that Serena would not have done this unless she saw something in you that I knew already existed," said my mother.

"I suppose," I said with a look of doubt.

"Emily," said my mother, lifting my face to hers. "It's okay to feel that doubt. You feel it because you never want to let anyone down. You never want to disappoint those you care about. And I want you to trust me and listen to what I have to say at this moment and never forget," said my mother.

"What?" I said listening intently.

"No matter what you do and no matter what happens, your father and I along with Cy and Ms. Pike will always love you," said my mother, looking down at Lilly sleeping. She continued, "Family is forever, no matter how long forever maybe."

I hugged my mother and gently kissed Lilly's forehead. As I watched Lilly sleep, I had forgotten what it felt like when my mother could peer into your soul and just know what it needed. Then I recalled my dream with Serena and wondered if she too, like my mother, knew what I needed. Making my way out of the nursery, I stood in the doorway, lost in my thoughts for a few minutes. I turned my head back into the room and saw my mother push open the French doors and walk out onto the wooden balcony. It was then a small creeping smile grew onto my face. I had finally understood what both women were trying to tell me. It was in that moment I knew how I was going to save Sam. However, I needed some time in my father's library to work out more of the details. I had a couple hours before the prep meeting with my father and Cy, so I headed for the library. I searched through most of my father's ancient books. During my search, I noticed some books were already pulled from the shelves. I assumed my father had already combed through these pages. But I needed to know more about Sam's curse. I pulled a book on ancient witch curses that I seemed to be drawn to. Flipping through the pages I skimmed over each section until I came to one part of the book that talked about curse removals. As I read through the passage, hope for my plan soon began to dwindle. I pulled another book, hoping to get a different answer. However, each book I pulled on curse removal all said the same thing: "Only the one who first bestowed the curse shall remove it. Magic, even the strongest of magic, can try, yet it may only to lead to death upon the one who bears the curse." What I feared the most seemed to be the only way I could save Sam. If I used the Jade Crystal to remove Sam's curse, there is a chance that I could end up losing Sam forever. I closed all the books and shook my head. *I am not willing to do that. I can't*, I thought.

—⚏—

Cy was also up early working in his lab preparing for the extraction of the crystal and its vault casing. He was proud of his new creation and he was anxious to show it off at the preparation meeting. Cy glanced at his watch expecting the others to arrive shortly. Since the elevators were still in repair from the attacking wolves, Daniel used the back stairwell to meet Cy in the lab.

"When are you not working on something down here?" said Daniel, walking into the lab.

"I will stop working when we stop getting ourselves into particular life-or-death, save-the-world situations that don't require me to work on something," said Cy.

Daniel laughed. "That would mean not anytime soon," he added.

"Precisely, so let's get to work, shall we. Where's Emily? I have something to show her," said Cy.

"I'm sure she is on her way. I see you have been working on the vault casing," said Daniel.

"Yes, I have!" exclaimed Cy with pride.

Daniel smiled and applauded, feeding Cy's ego just in time for Emily's arrival.

—⚏—

"What did I miss?" I asked seeing my father praising Cy.

"I was just about to demonstrate what I created for the artifacts," said Cy with uncontrollable enthusiasm.

My father and I watched as Cy began his demonstration of the new vault. Cy's idea for the vault casing stemmed from the disks used to create the invisible transportation device used on Rick back in the woods. He modified the disks to create a smaller spherical bubble around the gem. The bubble's shield was like Sam's containment door. Nothing could get in, and anything inside would simply deflect off the sides. The gem would not only be safe from anyone who could use it but also be transportable.

"Wow, that's amazing!" I said, noticing the gem within the demonstration. "Where did you get that?" I asked.

"Good observation, Emily. Well, I created that fake crystal with my replicating device. It's finally completed. The device was a success. As you can see, a very clever replica of the original crystal, strictly for prop purposes of course," said Cy, boasting with pride.

"Brilliant as usual, Cy," added my father.

"Emily, now let me show you what I have for you," said Cy, presenting a tiny flat black dot he loaded into a small injector.

"What is that?" I asked.

"It's a wireless—plus waterproof—earpiece. The range on this device is remarkable," said Cy, pulling me closer to him. "It's specifically designed to fit behind your ear rather than inside. When I place the injector behind your ear, you will feel some pressure, so try and stay still," said Cy, putting the injector in place.

The injector felt cold to my skin, and as Cy pressed the release button, I tried to not move. Once I felt the pressure behind my ear, I heard Cy say it was done. I instantly felt the area the earpiece was placed. I couldn't believe how flat it felt, almost like a small piece of confetti stuck to my skin.

"Okay, let's run a test. Go ahead, Emily, say something," said Cy, moving to the brain table.

"Test one, two. Can you hear me from this teeny tiny device?" I said, hearing my voice echo through the lab.

"Sound is good here. I have also added another feature. Tap the earpiece twice," said Cy, nodding to my father.

I tapped the earpiece, and within seconds, a small blue-screen-like lens popped into view over my right eye.

"What is this?" I asked with excitement.

"If there is something you need to show me, this lens will project whatever you see onto the brain table," said Cy.

I moved my head around the lab, and as I did, shots of what I saw came into view onto the brain table's screen.

"Very nice," I said.

"To remove the lens, just tap on the earpiece once," said Cy.

I tapped on the earpiece as instructed, and the lens was gone.

"Emily, how's the sound on your end?" asked my father.

I looked at my father. "I'm standing right here, of course I can hear you," I said, laughing.

"Good point. Go into the other room and close the door. We can do the sound test on your end from there," said Cy.

I giggled and locked myself into the other room.

"Okay, what about now, how is your sound?" asked my father again.

I was amazed how clear I heard him. If I didn't know any different, I would say he was right next to me. "All clear on my end," I replied.

When I rejoined my father and Cy in the lab, the two men were discussing who was going to join me on this expedition. We had initially decided on Sam and Father, but now with Sam gone and my new baby sister born, it seemed clear especially to me what would be the best solution.

"I think I should do this on my own," I said, interrupting the two men.

"What? No!" said my father.

"You need to stay here with Mom and Lilly. And you, Cy, need to monitor me from the lab. I'm at my cove. I have gone there by myself for months. Today will be no different," I said convincingly.

"She has a point, Daniel," said Cy.

"What if something happens to you in the cave? You won't have any backup," said my father.

"Cy, did you put a tracking system on my earpiece? I asked.

"Of course!" said Cy.

"See, Cy is my backup," I said.

"Again, I concur with Emily," said Cy.

"Cy, you are not helping," said my father, growing agitated.

"Father, I know you are worried. But I know I can do this. I need to do this," I said with certainty.

My father looked at me and sighed. "When your mother finds, out make sure you tell her whose idea it was," said my father. "And I'm proud of you," he added with a quick wrap of his arms around me.

"Well, now that we have resolved that matter, I have a couple more DES items I want you to have, Emily," said Cy.

Cy handed me a thin bag that contained a small air-breathing canister good for forty-five minutes to one hour, a small flat crowbar-looking object, and a small flashlight.

"Cy, these look like ordinary items. What do I do with them?" I asked, waiting for his technological explanation.

"Oh, well, you breathe into the canister if you need air, use the flat part of the bar to pry the gem from the rock, and use light if its dark," said Cy.

I gave Cy a puzzled glance. "So, no special designs or modifications?" I asked.

"Nope. Well, the bag is waterproof, but it just came that way," said Cy.

"Okay, then I am all set," I said, getting ready to leave the lab.

Just as I was heading toward the back stairwell, my father joined me.

"I know you can handle this, Emily. As your father, it is hard for me to not be there to protect you," said my father.

"I know. But you also told me that sometimes, you can only go so far and then the rest is up to me," I added.

My father smiled not just from pride of knowing his wisdom was becoming legacy but also from the reassurance in my growing confidence.

"Then be careful. You were right, we are in the race. I can only hope you get there first," said my father.

As we reached the main level, I agreed with my father, and we parted ways. On my way to my room to change, I thought of Sam. I knew he would never put me in danger on purpose. And I could only hope that he would try and give me the time I needed. Yet I wondered what he would have to risk to do that.

Chapter

22

Sam awoke in the cell no longer in his wolf form. He found clothes next to him to change into. Rick was nowhere to be found, and as he pushed on the cell door, he noticed it was not locked. *Could this be my chance to escape?*

Sam pushed the cell door open completely and started toward the staircase. As he ascended, he could hear muffled voices the closer he reached the top. The closer he got to the top the voices were recognizable.

"He knows more than you think" said Rick.

"What does he know?" said Zara.

"I am not sure, but I have a gut feeling it has to do with the crystal you keep talking about," said Rick.

"Hmmm. That's interesting. How would he know of it?" questioned Zara.

"I have no idea," said Rick.

"Maybe I should ask him?" said Zara.

"I have a feeling he won't be too talkative. You may have to force it out of him," said Rick.

"You are right. Maybe force is better. Come, we go to him now," said Zara.

Sam could hear their footsteps draw closer. Trapped on the stairs, Sam saw a way to sneak by them and hurried to the top step. The door flew open, and in walked Rick and Zara, descending to the lower level. Squished up between the wall and the door of the very top step, Sam found a small crevasse to hide. As Rick and Zara descended lower toward the basement, Sam quickly slipped out the door way and into the cabin. Sam scanned the cabin for a way out. He knew if the other wolves were outside, he wouldn't be able to outrun them in human form, so he looked for another option. That option presented itself as a set of car keys laid on the table. Sam scooped up the keys and climbed out one of the cabin windows to the Jeep parked out back. The wolves were all gathered on the porch. Sam was able to get into the Jeep, start the engine, and steer the Jeep into one of the bigger paths leading into the woods. Sam planned to get to the main road once he cleared the cabin through the back-forest roads. Once he was free, he would be able to meet up with Emily at the cove and help her find the crystal. As Sam drove through the woodsy path, he constantly looked behind to see if he was being followed, but there was no one. Sam finally made it to the main road and with a sigh of relief; he felt as though he had kept Emily and the rest safe from Zara. The main road was paved, which allowed Sam to increase the Jeep's speed toward freedom. Sam smiled knowing along this black road way divided by a yellow line would be his way out. Yet freedom would come at a price as the Jeep's increasing speed suddenly collided with an enormous black mountain of fur that ran out onto the road. As Sam quickly swerved to avoid the animal, a blanket of black feathers covered his windshield. Sam could not see a thing, nor could he control the Jeep that was now spinning out of control. The spinning led to it toppling over and rolling into the trees off the road. The big black bird with a purple stripe along its side landed on top of the wreckage while the black wolf pulled Sam's injured body from the wreck and dragged him to the side of the road.

Lying on the pavement, Sam opened his eyes to find Zara in human form looking down at him. Helpless and afraid, Sam thought only of Emily. "Forgive me, Emily," he whispered gently.

"You will tell me what you know," said Zara waving her hand over Sam's head and began to chant.

I arrived at my cove early so I could witness the water reach its lowest point and reveal the cave's entrance. The morning was sunny and warm with a cool breeze that blew off the water occasionally. It was warm enough to just have a thin cap-sleeved swim shirt over my two-piece bathing suit. Dressed in my gear, I sat perched on my small beach as I would usually do and waited. It felt different to be back here. What drew me to my cove in the beginning all those months ago was the need to find answers. I thought, *The day I met Sam, saved his life, and awoke the magic inside me was the day that started the chain reaction toward finding these answers.*

Now that I have the answers, I am drawn back here with purpose. I couldn't help but think about what Serena said about the crystal being bound to her for eternity and now the same is to be for me. If that is true, then this cove was more than just a coincidental find on my part; maybe the cove found me. I watched as the waves continuously broke over the rocks, and with each break, I noticed the water level lower as more of the rock's entirety became exposed. When I glanced over in the cave's direction, I could see the entrance slightly becoming revealed. I looked down at my watch and noticed it was just a few minutes before 11:00 a.m. Soon, the entrance was going to be completely revealed. Realizing it was time, I checked in with Cy on the com-link. "Cy, can you hear me?"

"I read you loud and clear, Emily, what is your status?" asked Cy.

"The water level has lowered, and I'm just about to swim to the cave's entrance now," I said.

"Copy that. Give me an update when you get to the cave's entrance," said Cy.

"Will do," I said turning off my com-link.

I made my way into the water and swam toward the cave's entrance. With the lowered tide, the currents were not as strong, which made the swim easier. When I reached the cave's entrance, I climbed onto its rocky ledge. The opening was narrow but wide enough for me to fit. Once I made my way through the opening and walked a few feet through a rocky corridor, the cave opened into a place of hidden splendor. I turned on my com-link and the eye lens to give Cy a view of what I was seeing.

"Cy, can you see this?" I said, pivoting my head to give a clearer view.

"Where are you?" asked Cy.

"I'm inside the cave," I said.

I entered a rock formed like circular room that had a pool of water in the middle while around it, a solid ledge encompassed the pool. As I glanced around the ledge, I could see three other entrances embedded in the cave walls. You could walk around the ledge to enter these openings. I pulled out my flashlight to see how high the cave walls stood. I lifted my eyes to the top and could see the cave walls did have a ceiling. I realized that during high tide, this room would easily be underwater, and anyone caught inside during this time could be trapped. I flashed the light unto the walls of the cave to see if there was evidence of the crystal. After searching all the walls, I noticed there was no sign of the crystal being embedded anywhere in this room's walls.

"I don't see the crystal in this room," I said.

Then I glanced over at the other entrances; I had to choose. I walked up to each entrance and shone my light into each of them; all of them seemed the same. The hallway into each entrance was dark and long. Not knowing how far or where each entrance would go, the possibility of checking out each one seemed unlikely especially since I had a short window of time until low tide ended.

"Which one do I choose?" I asked Cy.

"The topographical scan I did earlier on the area shows each tunnel leads off in different directions. Your guess is as good as mine," said Cy.

I walked past each entrance, trying to figure out how to choose. As I stood in front of the middle entrance, I had this unexplainable draw to the darkness within. It felt as if I was being pulled into the darkness of the middle entrance like a magnet being pulled to a piece of metal. Something was drawing me into this entranceway and making the choice for me; I had to follow.

"Cy, I have a feeling about this entrance. I am going to check it out," I said, moving into the tunnel.

"Be careful, Emily," said Cy.

Guided by only my flashlight and a magnetic pull, I walked down a winding pathway. After walking for several minutes, I wondered if I was going to come to a room like the one I had left. As the path came to its last bend, I could see a faint glow of light at the end.

"What is that?" asked Cy, referring to the light.

When I finally reached the end of the path, I was able to witness what caused the light; it was sunlight. The end of the path brought me to a side entrance to an old well. The rocky walls led down to the bottom of the well still full of water, while above the rock walls led to a stone base opening where sunlight came through. Across my entrance, I noticed how the sunlight particularly beamed onto a certain part of the wall. Like a single spotlight onto a darkened stage, there it was, the Jade Crystal.

"How am I going to get across the well to that side of the wall?" I asked Cy.

"I guess I should have packed you more DES equipment," replied Cy.

"Yeah, a rope or climbing gear would be great right now," I added.

Just as I was in the middle of trying to figure out my current dilemma, I heard a strange sound echo from the pathway tunnels behind me.

"What is that sound, Emily?" asked Cy, overhearing it from the com-link.

I listened intently. "Sounds like water," I replied.

The sound of the water grew louder and almost thunderous like it was coming through the pathway at great force. I looked down at my watch and noticed it was slightly past noon.

"The tide was not due to change for another few hours," said Cy with concern.

"I have a bad feeling about this, Cy," I added.

Something else was forcing the water through the pathways, and I was stuck in the middle of its inevitable course. I only had a matter of seconds to make a choice, but it was too late. Water rushed through the pathway with such force I was swept off the ledge by a strong wave. The wave emptied into the well, sending my body to the bottom.

"Emily!" crackled Cy's voice in the com-link.

As soon as I hit the water below, my eye lens turned off. When I surfaced, I began treading, hoping to regain my connection with Cy.

"Cy, can you hear me?" I said, tapping on my earpiece.

Cy's voice was intermittent. The force of the wave disrupted our connection.

I watched as the well began to fill up. I figured as the well filled up, I would just ride the rise of the water all the way up to the crystal. While treading, I suddenly started to feel another magnetic pull, this time, toward the bottom of the well. I had to know why or what was the draw to the bottom, so I pulled out the air canister and dove down. The base of the well was not rock but rather sand. When I scanned over the bottom, I could see something buried beneath the sand. Without thinking, I just grabbed it and headed for the surface, hoping not to miss my window to free the crystal. As I quickly swam to the top, I opened my bag to place the new object in it and grab the bar to use on the crystal. The water had risen quickly. By the time I reached the surface, I was already at the crystal's location and water had filled the well from the side entrance. I wedged the bar into the rock where the gem rested and attempted to pry it free. Each attempt was futile. The gem would not budge from its spot. The water kept pouring in and was slowly rising above where I worked on trying to free the crystal. I would soon have to pry it free underwater. The well was more than half full. While I worked tirelessly still trying to obtain the crystal, I had lost track of how long I was submerged. When I finally looked down at my air canister, I could see my air was getting very low and still the gem had not budged. Frustrated and afraid of being trapped, I slammed my palm onto the face of the gem. As soon as my palm connected with the crystal, I could feel a flow of energy I have never felt before. My hand was stuck to the crystal; it felt magnetized. I was being pulled into the gem, and it was being pulled into me; we were connected. The longer I stayed connected, the more of my air was being used. I closed my eyes and held the energy from the crystal. Instead of visualizing an image to allow the magic to happen, this time, I simply spoke words in my mind.

Release, I thought.

Just as the word left my mind, I could feel myself pull away from the rock wall. As I floated away, I looked down at my hand to happily see what I came here for. We were both free. But my air canister was now empty. I quickly struggled to swim to the surface. Once I reached the top, I broke the water, gasping for air with the crystal in hand. When

I looked up at the well's opening that seemed several feet above me, a shadow had blocked some of the sunlight. I saw two figures standing over the opening, and then a voice called down to me.

"Give us the crystal and you will live," said the voice of a man.

"No! I can't," I replied, slightly out of breath and still treading water.

"Then you will die. We will get the crystal from your dead watery corpse," said the voice of a woman.

As the shadows moved away from the opening, I heard what sounded like stone grinding against stone. The light from the opening was growing smaller and smaller until it was no more. They had covered the opening, leaving me trapped in the well all alone.

—⟋⟋⟍—

Back at the lab, Cy desperately tried to regain his connection to Emily. He tracked her last known whereabouts and activated the tracker on her. The signal was faint but still worked, which means Emily was in an area exposed to open air somehow. Cy began to trace her last location and the possible areas she would be based on the different pathways each tunnel led to. Only one area that seemed to lead to an open airway was the one that lead to the old forgotten well a mile from the cove. He quickly gathered his things and left to find Emily.

—⟋⟋⟍—

I looked around at the walls of the well. I found a small ledge to hold on to. This allowed me to take a break from treading water at least until I could figure out what to do next. I realized who the voices belonged to; the male voice was Rick's, and I can only assume the woman's voice was Zara's. Realizing Zara was present now explained the rise in the tide. Her magic had trapped me. Looking above at the closed opening, I gathered that would be my only way out. However, I also knew what would be facing me on the other side. I looked down at the Jade Crystal and decided on another choice. I placed the crystal between my hands, reconnected with the crystal's energy, and spoke the answer to my dilemma.

Stairs, I thought.

The crystal began to glow, and as it did, I saw the rocks embedded in the walls begin to protrude out into a winding staircase formation, leading up toward the opening. Even the small ledge I held on to slowly moved out to become larger so I could climb up on to it. When the magic of the crystal concluded, my escape from the well was revealed. All that was left was the stone covering the well.

"What do they see in this girl? She is weak and useless. Soon, the crystal will be mine," said Zara with a devilish grin.

"I agree. When I first met her in the woods, there was nothing special about her. I don't understand why Sam would try so hard to protect her," said Rick, leaning on the well's stone covering.

Suddenly, the sound of cracking echoed. Rick and Zara looked about to see where the sound was coming from. The cracking sound grew louder and even more distinct. It was then they realized it was coming from the stone that covered the well.

"What is making this happen?" asked Zara.

"I am not sure," said Rick, backing away from the stone.

Both Rick and Zara watched from a distance the sudden explosion of the stone into pieces. The blast was loud and powerful enough to send pieces of rock soaring into the air and barely missing them as they landed. When the barrage of falling rocks subsided, a cloud of dust hovered over the well's opening. When the dust cleared, the person Rick and Zara once thought to be useless and weak now became their biggest threat.

Racing through a path that led to the old well, Cy heard an explosion. Concerned for Emily's safety he raced to the well. He had arrived at the place just in time to see Emily emerge from a cloud of dust. Rick and Zara watched in awe as a water saturated Emily stood before them carrying her water bag across her chest and something in her hand.

"Emily!" whispered Cy, feeling relieved that she was safe and unharmed.

Cy kept his distance but tried to regain com-link with her.

"Emily, it's Cy. I am on your six. Do you read?" whispered Cy as to not alert Rick and Zara.

"Copy that. Hold and wait for me," I replied, feeling reassured that I now have backup should my next plan go sideways.

"Who are you, girl, and how did you do that?" asked Zara with intense curiosity.

"My name is Emily. I have something you want. And you have something I want,"

"It was impossible to escape from the well. How did she do that?" asked Rick with a glance at Zara.

"I sense magic in you, girl. Why did I not sense this before? And why do I sense something else very familiar about you?" questioned Zara.

"Who I am does not matter. You came for this, did you not?" I said, revealing the Jade Crystal in my palm.

Zara's eye widened and then instantly narrowed all in one movement.

"I could kill you right here for it," said Zara.

"You can try, but you know that with this in my possession, killing me would prove difficult," I said.

Yet Zara wasn't convinced. She rubbed her hands together and thrust her palm into Rick's chest. Rick transformed into wolf form and ran toward my direction.

I held the crystal in one hand, and as the wolf leaped toward my face, I lifted my other hand with my palm facing out and yelled, "Shield!"

As if running into a wall, the wolf was deflected and flew back, unable to continue his attack on me. The wolf lay on the ground, whimpering from the collision. Zara watched in frustration as her biggest weapon lay wounded.

"We can do this all day, or we can discuss terms. Your choice?" I said, hoping now Zara would be convinced.

"Very well. We talk terms. What do you want from me?" said Zara, crossing her arms in defiance.

"I want Sam back. You give me Sam in exchange for the crystal," I said.

Zara looked at me with disbelief. "Why is he so important to you?" she asked.

"He just is," I demanded.

"Hmm, you care about this boy Sam. And I see now why he tried to protect you. He cares for you too," said Zara, nodding her head.

"Do we have a deal?" I persisted.

"How do I know you will honor our arrangement?" asked Zara.

"You don't. You will just have to take me on my word and trust," I said.

Zara laughed. "Little girl, I have no trust for anyone or anything. But I will give you back your Sam for the crystal. This I will do," said Zara.

"Fine. At dusk tomorrow, we will meet at Rick's ranger station for the exchange. If Sam is harmed in any way, the deal is off. Are we clear?" I concluded.

"We are clear. Dusk tomorrow. I will see you again little girl," said Zara as she shape-shifted into a big black bird and flew off.

As the bird flew away, I noticed the purple stripe along its side and watched as the wolf followed it into the woods.

The deal was done. The plan was set. And as Cy came out from the bushes, his facial expression said it all. "Emily, I hope you know what you are doing?" he muttered.

Chapter

23

When Zara arrived at Rick's cabin, she went directly down the winding staircase to the lower level where Sam lay resting in his cell.

"Who is she? Who is this Emily really?" asked Zara, enraged.

Sam awoke abruptly feeling caught off guard by Zara's temper.

"What do you mean? She is just a girl I met a few days ago," said Sam, sitting up and crawling into the corner of his bed.

"She is no ordinary girl. There is more to her that I did not see. Tell me," said Zara, growing even more persistent.

"There is nothing to tell," said Sam, still trying to keep Emily's identity a secret.

"Now pain will bring truth," said Zara as she reached for Sam's head and wrapped her fingers around his temples.

Sam shrieked in pain and fell onto his mattress. Zara continued to probe, searching for the truth, but Sam was unbreakable. Until one last jolting probe revealed the link to the person she sought to find when she was first freed from her prison and the only person who knew where to find the Jade Crystal.

"Serena!" cried Zara.

Flashes of who Emily truly was and how her magic was born flooded Zara's mind. She wanted to probe more, but Sam's body was weakening, and she had to keep him alive to obtain what she truly wanted. Sam could not be collateral damage, she thought, and released her hold on him. Yet the more she thought about how he could be used to serve her purpose, the more the idea of being less of a bargaining chip and possibly more of a pawn seemed to make her smile.

When Cy and I finally arrived back at the mansion, it was midday. We all gathered in the study for a debriefing. I knew my plan was not going to be accepted by my father and least not by my mother. My father would never accept the risk I was about to take, and my mother would not want to fathom the danger. But I knew what I was doing. I could only hope that they would trust that.

"You did what?" shouted my father.

"I agreed to trade the crystal for Sam," I said, expecting more yelling.

"Where and when is this exchange supposed to take place?" asked my father, trying to stay calm yet failing.

"Rick's ranger cabin at dusk," added Cy.

"What were you thinking, Emily?" said my father, growing even more furious with me.

"I was thinking the only way to get Sam back was to use the one thing Zara wanted the most. This is the only way," I said.

"Emily, you realize Zara will scheme to betray you and then come at you with her wolf army led by Rick?" said my father.

"I realize that. That's why you and Cy need to come up with a way to find a weakness against the wolves. While I deal with Zara," I added.

"I hate to say this but—" said Cy

"Don't you say it Cy—" interjected my father.

"But Emily makes a good point," said Cy.

My father lifted his arms in the air and pointed his finger at Cy. "I told you not to say it,"

"Daniel, hostile emotions aside, you know Emily is right. If we can figure out a way to disarm the wolves, that gives us more of a fighting chance to save Sam," said Cy, trying to bring reason back to conversation.

"What is all the commotion? Lilly can hear you all shouting from her room," said my mother, hobbling into the study, still recovering from her surgery.

"Emily made a deal with Zara to give her the crystal in exchange for Sam. The exchange is to happen tomorrow at dusk at Rick's ranger cabin," informed Cy.

My mother looked at my father and then looked at me. "Is that the only way we can get Sam back?" she asked.

"It's our best option at this point," said Cy.

My mother pensively paused and said, "Then that's what we do,"

"You are agreeing with this?" asked my father.

"Sam is family. If it was any one of you, I am sure we would be doing the same thing," said my mother.

I looked at my mother in disbelief and then at my father, who also looked dumbfounded, but we all knew her wisdom was irrefutable.

"Excellent because I may have an idea to handle the wolves. So, I will head down to the lab and get working on it," said Cy leaving the room.

"And I think I should get cleaned up. Sounds like a hot shower is calling my name," I said, pretending to leave the room.

I knew my parents needed some alone time to talk, but my curiosity kept me within listening distance behind a slightly cracked open door.

"You know I don't like this plan," said my father.

"I know. And it's because you never thought of it," said my mother.

"There are too many variables, too many things that can go wrong," added my father with concern.

"But there are also many things that can go right if you plan accordingly. And you know that is what you are best at doing," said my mother, understanding his worry.

"I can't be there to protect her especially when she faces Zara. I am not sure how to do this as a mortal," said my father, covering his face with his hands in frustration.

"Stop thinking about what you cannot do for her and focus on what you can do for her," said my mother as she pulled his hands away from his face and stared into his eyes.

"And what is that? What can I do for her?" asked my father, deeply focusing on my mother's gaze.

"Trust her, believe in her, fight alongside her, and let her take the lead. We are what makes her strong. We are her tether to this world even though she is immortal," said my mother.

"You know about her mortality? Did she tell you?" asked my father with a surprised look.

"No. she didn't tell me. I figured it out. We need to let her go and be who she needs to be. Can you do that?" asked my mother, gently caressing the side of his face with her palm.

My father stared into my mother's eyes and, with a loving smile confessed, "How did I get so lucky to have you?" pulling her into his arms, grateful for reminding him of what he already knew in his heart to be true.

As I witnessed my father and mother's bond with each other, I came to realize how lucky I was to have them both in my life.

As I left my parents in the study, I walked up to the stairs, and before heading to my room I stopped by Sam's room. As I looked around his room, I saw his clothes my mother got for him still folded neatly on the dresser and the bag he used on the camping trip. I grabbed the bag and filled it with some of his clothes. *Sam is coming home,* was my only thought. I closed the door and walked toward my room.

The shower helped me to sort out my thoughts. I knew how to handle Zara, but I still had not worked out the final solution for Sam. I was conflicted still. As I stepped out of the shower, a familiar voice who I had hoped to talk to called out my name. As per our usual communication, I walked over to the mirror and waited for Serena to appear.

"Emily, I sense you are troubled," said Serena.

"Yes. It's Sam," I said.

"I see. Then let me take you back to the time when I first met your father," said Serena.

"He told me about that time. He said he saved your life," I said.

"Yes, he did. And in return, I gave him another life. A life he deserved to have even though he too was cursed," said Serena.

"See, that's what I cannot understand. Why didn't you remove the curse for him?" I asked.

"Curses can only be removed by the one who bestowed it. I did not give your father the curse, Gideon did," said Serena.

As I began to recall the events from the catacombs, I realized my father's transformation from immortal to mortal was Gideon's doing. And since he bestowed the curse, he was able to remove it with magic used from the book of Mystics and the medallion.

"It all makes sense now. But how does this help me with Sam?" I asked.

"Emily, your father's humanity allowed me to alter his curse by giving him a soul. You can use Sam's humanity to do the same," said Serena.

"Serena I still don't understand," I said shaking my head.

"You will when the time comes. You now have everything you need, Emily. Your time is now," said Serena.

As Serena's image slowly began to fade, her words, "Your time is now," repeated over and over until my image came into view in the mirror.

When I walked out of my bathroom and into my room, I noticed the water bag hanging on the chair next to my bed. I unzipped the pocket I had placed the Jade Crystal in and took it out. Staring down at the crystal, I recalled the image of Serena being lifted above the floor of the vault by the swirling wind as the crystal circled her.

There is no much power here, I thought holding the gem in my palm.

Just as I was about to return the gem back into the pocket, I had remembered the other item I grabbed from the well's bottom. I pulled the sides of the bag wide apart, creating an opening large enough to see what it was. When my eyes gazed upon its golden shape and glowing ruby-red gem, I truly believed Serena when she said I had everything I needed. Laid upon my bed were the two long lost artifacts of Avalon's Vault.

Chapter

24

The dawn, with its red hue painted between the clouds, came and went without me even noticing. I had slept in for most of the morning hours. These last couple nights of restlessness finally caught up to me. I rose from my pillow and pulled out the Jade Crystal from my bag and held it once again in my palm. Its weight was light, its texture was smooth with the edges so finely carved out. The longer I held it, the more I could feel its power. It was the same feeling I experienced in the well. The thought of Zara feeling this same power not only scared me but also left me with a sinking feeling of terror. But the deal was made, and it was made for a reason. It was made to get Sam back. And that would be my only goal.

My father and I spent the entire day going over our plan of action. From the moment I awoke to the midafternoon hours, we were in his study, hammering out our plan to get Sam back. We knew everything had to be precise and carefully thought out. The only concern we had left to deal with was leaving my mother, Ms. Pike, and Lilly home alone, defenseless, should the meeting not go as planned.

"We can call Dr. Elliot for backup?" I said to my father.

"That's a good idea. I would be comfortable with at least having someone here. I'll make the call now," said my father, pulling out his phone.

After a few minutes of chat with Dr. Elliot, my father ended is phone conversation, and I probed for an answer. "What did he say?"

"He said he would be happy to help out. He has a late appointment today and will come directly to the house afterward. So, we are all set there," said my father.

With that last part of the plan in place, Cy's voice echoed from the intercom, calling us both to help him with his idea to handle the other wolves. My father and I left his study and made our way to the lab. When we arrived at the lab, we noticed large speaker-like devices lying in the middle of the lab floor and Cy intensely working on them.

"What are these for?" I asked.

"It's our best defense against the wolves," replied Cy.

"You plan on lulling them to sleep with music?" I asked trying, to lighten the mood.

"Not quite. You will see. I just need you both to help me lift these onto the Jeep," said Cy with stern authority.

All three of us lifted the device up and made our way through the back stairwell.

While hauling, Cy confessed, "Yes, I will work on fixing the elevator next," missing the convenience of mechanical transportation between levels.

"I am going to hold you to that," said my father, lifting the heavier end of the device.

Reaching the main level, we headed out through the front entrance where the Jeep was parked.

"Accounting for travel time, we should leave here within a couple hours," said Cy while mounting the device unto the Jeep.

"Agreed," added my father.

"I will meet you all back here at the Jeep by then," I said, heading back into the house leaving my father and Cy to their mechanical endeavors.

—〰—

"How did your planning session go with Emily?" Cy asked Daniel as he finished tightening a screw to his device.

"It went well. I think we have all the bases covered," replied Daniel as he handed Cy another screw to fasten.

"You know, if things do go sideways, Emily is the only big gun we have," added Cy.

"I know. And I think she knows that as well," said Daniel.

"Do you think she is ready?" asked Cy.

"I have to trust that she is," replied Daniel, glancing at his old friend with sincerity and truth.

The next couple hours were spent in my room going over the plan in my mind. I tried to find little things to distract me, but deep down, all I wanted was for time to speed up. I thought about using the Phoenix Staff to transport me to the cabin sooner, but I knew for everything to play out as we wanted it to, every detail had to be executed at its precise moment. And the use of Phoenix Staff had not reached its moment. So I took my time packing and picking out my clothes I needed for tonight. I decided to continue to use the water bag Cy gave me because it proved useful. And when it was finally time, I grabbed Sam's bag and headed back downstairs to wait by the Jeep. Just as I was coming down the staircase, I was met at the bottom by my mother, Ms. Pike, and Lilly.

"We wanted to wish you luck," said my mother, leaning Lilly into me for a kiss.

I gently kissed Lilly's little head and gave my mother a quick snuggle.

"Dearie, you take care of yourself," said Ms. Pike, handing me a bag of food.

I laughed at how Ms. Pike always had food for me.

I wanted to say that I was going to see them soon. And I wanted to let them know that Sam would be home soon too. But nothing came out. I could only nod and give them hugs.

"Your father and Cy are already waiting in the Jeep," said my mother.

"Okay," I finally said with yet another nod.

My mother watched as I walked toward the door. Passing Lilly off to Ms. Pike, she followed behind. "Emily!" called my mother.

I turned to meet her.

"Bring him back. I know you can," said my mother, referring to Sam.

"I'll do my best," I said.

And with that, I made my way to the Jeep and climbed into the back seat. I looked over at the empty seat beside me and remembered the last time I was in this Jeep; Sam sat there. I heard my father fire up the engine, and we were off down the driveway and soon on the road, heading toward Rick's ranger cabin.

During the drive, I sat quietly, listening to my father and Cy discuss each role for tonight. Cy had still not disclosed what his full plan was to deter the wolves. Though I am sure my father knew more of it than I did. Cy was confident it was going to work, and that was good enough for me.

"What about Rick?" I asked.

"If he is in human form, I will deal with him. And if he is in wolf form, Cy takes it from there," said my father.

"We only have a small window of time. If we get Sam away from Zara, we still need to deal with trying to contain him when he changes," said Cy.

"We have a plan for that," said my father.

"Cy, did you reset the shield doors to the containment room in your lab?" I asked.

"Yes, they are all set as per your request, Emily. And who's going to make the exchange?" Cy added.

"I will," said my father.

"And I'll wait to get Sam," I added.

"Sounds simple enough," said Cy.

"It's always simple in theory. It's just a matter of execution and whether Zara has plans of her own," said my father.

We knew to expect some type of deception from Zara and Rick. It was a game of chess. As they made their move, we would have to quickly counter with our own.

The Jeep pulled into the same parking lot paved by gravel stones it had visited just a few days before. It was dusk. We arrived on time; Zara and her army did not. Suddenly, we heard movement from the bushes from both sides of the cabin. It was Zara's wolves that were making their appearance. The wolves walked toward the cabin and stood in front, creating a barrier between us and the cabin.

"So, little girl, you do keep your word," said Zara, walking out through the cabin door with Rick in human form following behind.

Only my father and I exited the Jeep; Cy remained inside.

"I told you, you can trust me on that," I yelled back over to Zara.

"Daniel!" hollered Rick. "You're here too, I see," Rick taunted.

"Rick, I am here to make sure nothing happens to my daughter and we can get Sam back," said my father, moving to join my side.

"Where is Sam?" I hollered back.

"Where is the crystal?" Zara asked.

"It's right here," replied my father, holding the crystal up in the air. Zara walked down the porch steps to get a clearer look at the gem. She nodded and motioned to Rick.

"Go get the boy," Zara ordered Rick.

Rick went into the cabin and came back out with a very worn-out, broken-looking Sam, whose hands were bound by a with rope.

"Sam!" I gasped. "I told you if he was hurt the deal would be off," I shouted in anger.

"Don't worry, boy is fine," said Zara. "See, he can stand and walk," she said with a snicker.

"So, this is how we are going to do the exchange. I will bring the crystal to you once Sam is safe with us," said my father.

"No!" shouted Zara. "You will come halfway. Boy go halfway. When you meet in the middle, boy will continue to little girl. And you come to me with crystal. Little girl cannot have crystal near her. Agreed?" commanded Zara.

My father and I nodded to each other. "Agreed," said my father.

I watched as my father started to walk toward Zara and Rick. Just as he began his pace, Rick pushed Sam toward our direction down the porch steps. Both men walked as if heading to a duel, but in this case, there were no guns or weapons, just a pace to freedom.

As Zara instructed, the two men stopped halfway between both ends.

"It's going to be all right, Sam," whispered Daniel.

Sam moaned and continued to walk toward my direction. As he moved closer to me, my father started his pace toward Zara and Rick. The wolves that created a protection line in front of Zara slowly moved to allow my father's approach. As Sam was just a few paces from me, I saw his tired body almost begin to stumble. I raced to his side and allowed his weight to lean on me for support. My father looked back in my direction, and as our eyes met, he could see that Sam was now safe.

Relieved to know Sam would be safe, my father was just about to turn is attention back toward Zara's when an intense pain across his cheek caused by Rick's fist sent my father to the ground.

"Father!" I yelled from a distance.

"Sorry, Daniel. But it just needs to go down this way," said Rick grabbing the gem from his hand.

Zara opened her palm and lowered it toward Rick's direction. Rick looked up at Zara and, without hesitation gently laid the crystal to rest within her palm. Zara held the crystal between her hands and began a chanting whisper.

"Noctu egressus. Noctu egressus," Zara chanted into the crystal.

Zara's chant repeated over and over, growing louder and louder each time it was spoken. It was even loud enough for Cy to hear from the Jeep.

Cy listened to Zara's words carefully, recognizing the language. Under his breath, Cy repeated the words spoken by Zara over and over, trying to decipher the meaning of the chant. Finally, it came to him; it was Latin. *"Night come forth!"* Cy whispered.

Realizing what Zara was intending to do, Cy looked toward Emily. "Emily! Hurry get Sam into the Jeep!" cried Cy through the window.

Cy quickly opened his laptop and began to prepare his device. He was nearly ready with its setup, when suddenly, the wolves all leaped onto the Jeep. Cy could feel the crashing force of the animals on top of the roof. The Jeep shook violently as the pack drove their claws into every inch of metal they could mangle.

I saw my father slowly begin to awake on the ground and look up toward my direction. "Go, Emily! Go!" yelled my father.

Rick heard my father calling to me and moved to make another attempt to knock him out. But my father was quick enough to sweep Rick's legs, sending him to the ground this time. Zara continued to chant as if completely absorbed in the spell she was conjuring. I watched as Rick and my father were engaged in a fistfight turned wrestling match. Both men wrestled on the ground trying to pin the other. Punch after punch, Rick would gain a good shot at my father, and then my father would counter with a shot of his own. Both men were evenly matched in strength. However, it was my father who I knew had centuries of fighting skill that could best Rick in the end. I wanted to help my father, but I did what he asked: I hurried Sam to safety.

But where would be safe? I wondered, looking over at Cy trapped in the Jeep.

I managed to at least get Sam and I out of Zara's view and hidden behind a large tree. I would soon realize being safe was not going to be part of the plan. As I looked up at the sky, I truly understood the danger for all of us.

—m—

Dusk that left the sun sitting atop an orangey-red horizon was slowly changing. The sun was setting, and it was setting faster than usual, as if time were set on fast-forward. The couple hours of daylight Cy, Daniel and Emily calculated to have was erased; night was falling upon them. And as the black blanket of darkness came, so would the curse.

Zara stretched her arms out. "Now you will all witness what shall be your end and the beginning of my reign," she said with a commanding tone.

Daniel had just beaten Rick in their mortal fistfight. As Rick lay on the ground bleeding and holding his midsection, the night completed its arrival. Daniel knew his win over Rick would be short-lived, and although he had bested the man, he would now have to face the animal again. While on the ground, Rick moved to his hands and knees and, with a howling cry, ripped off his shirt, embracing his change. Daniel knew he had only seconds until the transformation was complete and saw this as a small window to lunge at Zara from behind, forcing the crystal out her hands an onto the ground.

"The crystal!" cried Zara, now calling upon her army to come to her aid.

The wolves left the Jeep and ran toward Daniel. Leaping to his feet, he managed to scoop up the gem and run into the woods drawing the wolves away from the cabin and Zara. However, the spell had been conjured, and the night had come. Rick's transformation was complete, and with a loud howl, he stood on the porch, calling to his pack to bring Daniel back here alive.

—∿—

When I looked back at Sam, he was already on the ground, curled up in a fetal position.

"Emily! Get out of here. I can't stop this," said Sam, trying desperately to keep the transformation at bay.

"No! I am not leaving. I am staying here," I said, kneeling down beside Sam.

Lifting himself to meet my eyes, Sam pleaded, "Then you need to end this before I hurt anyone. I can't stop them from controlling me. I can't stop Zara!" said Sam.

"I can't remove the curse, Sam. If I try, you will die," I pleaded.

My heart fell into my stomach as I wished not to hear the words I knew Sam was about to say.

"You promised, Emily. This is the only way to save everyone. I don't want to hurt anyone. You promised me," Sam said continuing to holler in pain.

I watched as Sam fought so hard to keep his transformation from consuming him. I could see the anguish in his eyes knowing that once he transformed, Zara would have him under her control. Zara would use him against me. I knew I only had a matter of seconds to make a choice. So I began to lay my hands onto Sam's chest, just like I did when we first met at the beach. I drew upon Sam's energy and began to feel the beat of his heart. My hands began to glow with a white brilliance I have never seen before. And as I held the glow, I could not hold back my tears from falling as I could feel Sam's energy slowly drain from his body. In that moment, with Sam's last heartbeat about to finish its final pulse, I knew what I had to do for Sam. My hands continued to glow brighter and brighter until there was a white flash. When the flash subsided, I could see that not only had I made the transformation stop, but I also made it so Sam would never transform again. I looked down at Sam.

He looked so peaceful and quiet. He was concealed from Zara and safe. I crossed his arms around his waist and whispered, "Rest now," wiping away the tears from my cheeks.

—⁂—

The wolves commanded by Rick emerged from the woods, dragging on the ground Daniel in their jaws.

"Daniel!" yelled Cy, finally free from the Jeep.

"I'm okay, Cy," replied Daniel feeling a bit banged up.

Cy stood at a distance, examining the exterior of the Jeep as the wolves all surrounded Zara and Rick. Zara bent down toward one of the wolves that held the crystal in its mouth. Zara freed the crystal from the animal's jaw and held it once again, ready to send yet another wave of her dark magic upon her enemies.

"Now where is little girl? Oh, little girl!" taunted Zara.

Emily came out from behind the tree that still concealed Sam. "Are you looking for me?" she asked.

"Ah, there you are. Now where is boy?" asked Zara.

"Sam is dead to you," I said.

Cy could not believe what he heard. "Sam is dead?" he whispered.

Zara laughed and asked, "You killed the boy?"

"I just kept a promise. That's all you need to know," Emily said, walking toward Zara.

"Well, I too will keep my promise. A vow I made to someone we both know very well. Tell Serena this world will be mine. And now with this," said Zara holding the crystal in the air, "I will have dominion over all. And no one can stop me."

"I don't believe that," Emily said sarcastically.

"I agree with my daughter. I don't think you have that much power," said Daniel with a smirk.

"I would like to second that," yelled Cy from the Jeep, noticing his device was still intact and ready.

"I turned day into night with the crystal in my command. That was great power!" said Zara.

"Yeah, that was okay. But I think I need to see more," said Daniel.

"I concur. Show us more! Show us more!" heckled Cy from the Jeep.

Zara began to chant, and as she did, the ground began to rumble and shake as she held the crystal. We all stumbled a bit from the unsettling movement of the earth, but the quake was short-lived.

"Is that all you got? You have the Jade Crystal. It has the power to enhance your magic by ten times its capacity. You can shape-shift into anything you want. As big as you want. Show us how big you can get!" Emily said, throwing the gauntlet down before her.

Zara yelled out of frustration and began to chant once again. This time as she chanted, she began to grow bigger and bigger, crashing into the porch's awning. The larger she grew, the quicker the wolves fled from her side as she now towered over the cabin and was high as the trees. Daniel also noticed his chance to run. He ran toward Cy and the Jeep. Yet what was she to become? They began to see the formation of giant wings and then a long tail starting to emerge from behind. From the front, they could see her head forming into a bird with birdlike talons while her back was more primal. What Zara became was something only someone from the mystical world could conjure. She was half bird and half lion.

"Well, that is big," said Cy from the Jeep.

—⟨⟨⟨⟩⟩⟩—

Zara began to flap her giant wings, creating a gust of wind around the cabin. The wind had such force it felt like as though we were hit by a windstorm. I flew back toward the Jeep, managing to grab hold of the hood, stopping me from flying into the air. I saw as my father and Cy also clutched to different parts of the Jeep.

"It can't be much longer now," I yelled.

"Look!" hollered my father.

We all watched as Zara, in her enormous animal form, started to walk toward the Jeep. As she drew closer, her wings were pulled back, stopping the windstorm. With the wind gone, we were able to release our hold on to the Jeep and regain our balance back on the ground. Yet, s one threat subsided, another stood towering above us. Zara let out a piercing squawk that echoed from her birdlike front. As Zara lifted her chest into air, I saw the crystal being held by her lioness tail behind her. Zara raised her front claw toward my direction, hoping to pin me by her giant talon, but she missed.

"Emily, be careful!" cried my father, watching the claw just missing my leg.

But Zara was not done with me yet. She attempted another swipe with her claws. I dove to the ground, but my escape wasn't successful. The tip of Zara's claw caught on to my bag and tore it from my shoulder. The bag fell to the ground, revealing my ruse. Zara carefully stared down at the small object that fell out of my bag. She looked back at her tail and then back at the ground. Before she could question anything, she began to feel dizzy and faint. Stumbling backward and away from the Jeep, Zara pulled in her giant wings to cover her body. Her cocoon-shaped figure began to gradually reduce in size. The real Jade Crystal had fallen out of my bag and lay a few inches from my hand.

"Cy! It's now or never," hollered my father.

With his laptop in hand, Cy activated the speaker-like devices. Within seconds, a strange high-frequency sound bellowed from the Jeep. The sound seemed harmless to human ears, but when we looked over at the wolves, they appeared to suffer more. The wolves that were just about to come to Zara's aid were stopped in their tracks by Cy's device.

"It's working!" cried Cy.

"Is that the garage door device?" asked my father.

"Yes, but modified," said Cy, watching as the smaller wolves' disoriented behavior stopped them from attacking.

The device worked like a sound barrier. The wolves were trapped behind it, cutting them off from Zara and the others.

Zara had now formed back into her human self. She watched as her call for help from her pack was futile. In a weakened state, she called out to Rick.

"Where's Rick?" I asked, noticing he was not with the other wolves.

Just as I was about to secure the real crystal, a large black paw pounced unto my arm, pinning it to the ground. Before I knew it, Rick, in his wolf form, was standing above me. Rick had heard Zara's call for help, and realizing our deception, he raced to obtain the real gem. Rick growled while his fangs stood inches from my face. Rick had a choice. He could use his fangs to grab the gem or drive them into me, hence transferring the curse to another. It was his instinctive primal anger that drove him to choose the latter.

"Emily!" cried out my father as Rick was about to plunge his fangs into me.

I screamed just before Rick's jaws were about to lunge into my head. I lifted my other arm, expecting to brace the impact and experience for the first time what it felt like to be mauled by an animal. But to my shock, none of that happened. Instead, I heard a voice calling out my name and then a human hand grab unto Rick's fur, pushing him away from me. At first I thought it was my father, but it wasn't him or Cy. The one who came to my rescue managed to launch the wolf far from me. I sat up, hoping to figure out who it was. The person that stood between me and wolf Rick was Sam. Sam in human form but different.

"Emily, grab the crystal and run!" said Sam as he prepared to take on another attack from Rick.

I grabbed the crystal, shoved it into my pocket, and ran toward the Jeep with Cy and my father. From a distance, we watched Sam continue the battle with Rick. Sam's movements were agile and animal-like. To our surprise, Sam was matching Rick's wolflike ability combat after combat. Sam also had unbelievable strength that was comparable to Rick's animal nature. But Rick was able to get one good shot in. Rick lunged at Sam with his sharp claw-like paws and created a gash on Sam's arm.

"Sam!" I cried, still watching the battle between man and animal.

Sam looked down at his wound and grew angry. Sam's flaring anger ignited another change. We watched as Sam's human nails suddenly began to grow into claws; now, Sam had weapons of his own. He rushed back at the wolf, swiping at him with his claws, luckily connecting with the animal's left leg. The wolf continued to charge at Sam. Sam leaped into the air, high enough to distract the wolf. On his descent, Sam landed on the wolf's back driving his claws into the wolf's sides. The wolf howled in pain. Sam now had a choice: end Rick's life or spare him. It was Sam's humanity that drove him to choose the latter. Sam leaped off the wolf's back and chose mercy.

"No!" cried Zara, who was soon realizing her dominion was coming to an end.

Still determined and with whatever strength Zara could muster, she transformed into a small gardener snake. Focused only on Sam's battle with Rick, I didn't see Zara slowly slither her way toward us. Gliding through the grass Zara moved between the blades and leaves until she found herself concealed by one of the Jeep's tire. It was there she waited until her moment.

I moved from the Jeep and stepped into an open area. "Sam!" I yelled, pulling out the Phoenix Staff from my bag.

With the staff in hand, I drew the circle of flames and motioned Sam to send Rick through the portal.

"Are you sure?" asked Sam.

"Yes! He will be contained. Trust me," I said.

Sam retracked his claws and moved toward Rick's wolf body lying on the ground. Just as he was about to launch the wolf into the ring of fire. The wolf sprung to his feet.

"Don't make me do this?" said Sam, not sure if the telepathic link was still there.

"I will not be a prisoner. I would rather die than live my life as if I was in one," said Rick telepathically.

Once Sam realized the telepathic link was still alive, he had to try and reach Rick somehow.

"It was Zara—she controlled you. You can break free from her," said Sam.

"Zara showed me a life I could have had with her. I can't go back to what I was before. I can't. I will not," replied Rick as he began to charge toward my direction and not toward the portal opening.

"Emily, get out of the way!" shouted Sam running toward me.

Rick's determination to obtain the crystal led him straight toward me at a fierce pace. I closed the portal to the containment room in Cy's lab and turned to run away from a charging wolf Rick. Just as I was about to the pull the crystal out of my pocket to defend myself, Sam flew into the air, trying to tackle Rick. While in midflight, Sam managed to grab hold of wolf Rick's neck just seconds before Rick's giant paw was about to swipe at my back. As man and animal crashed to the ground, Sam's strong hold on the wolf's neck accidently twisted, resulting in a slight cracking sound. In that split second, Rick's life—both man and animal—came to an end.

"I chose mercy. I didn't want this," said Sam sadly looking down at the still black mountain of fur before him.

I knelt down by the animal and placed my hand on its chest. I was hoping my magic could heal, but there was no energy force to bring back and no heartbeat to restore. Rick was never going to transform again. Death ended his curse.

"He is gone," I said, looking up at Sam.

"He chose this. He chose not to be prisoner anymore," said Sam dropping to his knees beside me.

"It was his choice to make," I said hoping to bring comfort to Sam.

"This is not how I wanted it to end," said Sam with remorse.

"I know," I said gently grabbing hold of Sam's hand.

Sam and I sat in silence to mourn a life lost then rose to our feet and together walked to rejoin my father and Cy by the Jeep.

"Sam, you are alive!" yelled Cy.

"Hmmm, well, apparently, I am," said Sam with a perplexed glance in my direction.

"Yes, I know. And I can explain. But first, what do we do with these wolves?" I asked.

"Those wolves were created by magic. They were human once. Zara's magic controls and traps them—forever being in animal form," said Sam.

Walking toward the area Zara was last seen, it occurred to me she was nowhere to be found. "Where is Zara?" I asked, finding only the fake crystal on the ground and placing it in my other pocket.

"Zara was weak, so she could not have gone far," Cy said.

We all fanned out to search for her.

But my father's first concern was for my mother and Lilly.

"Maybe Zara transformed into a bird. She could be anywhere. I need to call your mother and warn her," said my father as he stood by the Jeep, hoping to reach my mother on his cell phone.

As Daniel stood alone by the Jeep talking to Ellie on his cell phone, Zara decided it was time to seek revenge on the little girl who ruined her plans. Zara slithered away from the tire and moved behind Daniel where she shape-shifted back into her human form. Fueled by pure anger and hatred, Zara began to rub her hands together and chant. Zara then plunged her palm into Daniel's chest just as he was about to turn around.

———ɯ———

"Father!" I cried as I watched him fall to the ground and begin to convulse. My cry was heard by Sam and Cy, who both came running to my father's aid.

"What did you do to him?" I shouted while kneeling on the ground beside my father's body.

Zara fell to her knees before me. The last ounce of magic she was able to conjure up had truly weakened her physically. Yet her hatred for me continued to burn and ultimately consumed her.

"He becomes like them," said Zara, referring to the wolves she had created. "He is mine until my last dying breath," she added with a chilling devilish tone.

I watched as my father began to change just as I had seen Rick do the first time in the woods.

"I have taken something from you like you have taken from me, little girl," said Zara with a revengeful smile.

"Bring him back!" I commanded.

Zara laughed. "Give me the crystal. The real crystal and I will," she said, knowing she finally was going to get what she wanted.

No! I can't, I thought.

I looked down at my father moaning and wailing as the transformation was beginning to take form. Thoughts of my mother and Serena flooded my mind. I tried to recall all that they told me and all that I was supposed to do. It was then I realized I had a choice to make. I could lose my father forever, or I could give the crystal to Zara. What my father said once to me led me to choose the latter. I reached inside my pockets and pulled out both crystals. Staring at them for a moment, I bowed my head and then proceeded to lay them on the ground in front of Zara.

"Emily, what are you doing?" said Cy, witnessing my choice.

Zara glared at the two gems before her. Curious, she slowly crawled toward them and grabbed both from the ground.

"No!" gasped Sam, watching Zara hold both crystals in each of her hands.

"Now I get what I want. But how do I know which is true crystal?" said Zara, looking down at each crystal—one in the right hand and other in the left hand.

I looked back up at Zara and smiled.

"You are not supposed to know. Only I do," I said, grabbing hold of Zara's left hand.

Between the palms of our left hands, the real crystal was wedged. And as soon as my hand connected with the crystal, the magnetic force that once pulled me to it in the well secured my and Zara's hands together. We were locked in a magical bind.

"What is this?" asked Zara as she watched the Jade Crystal begin to give off a green glow.

"What it is bound to me for eternity and has the power to give magic will now take yours away," I said aloud, willing the thought and allowing the magic to flow.

Zara struggled to free herself from my grip, but it was useless. The more she struggled, the more the crystal continued to glow brighter, keeping her connected to me.

"How are you doing this?" said Zara, noticing the ground slowly moving away from us.

Caught in a green swirl of smoke, both Zara and I levitated into the air. The green swirl emanated from the crystal that held us both in its command. I grabbed hold of Zara's right wrist, keeping the fake crystal steady while we floated higher and higher.

"Stop this now!" Zara commanded.

But my focus was steady. And I was locked into the power of the crystal.

"Emily!" hollered Sam as we hovered now high above his head.

Yet the crystal was only doing what I had asked and would continue to until my request was completed. As the crystal completed stage one of its purpose, the green smoke slowly dissipated, and we began to lower to the ground. When we could feel the firmness finally below us, the crystal released its hold on the two of us. Zara finally was able to pull away from me, and I had control of both crystals once again. The real one was in my left hand, and in my right was the fake.

Zara began to cackle. "You see, your magic did not work. My strength has returned. I feel like myself again. I will destroy you!" Zara shouted as her words echoed throughout the trees.

"Just wait," I said with a calm yet commanding tone.

"Look!" yelled Cy.

"The wolves are changing," said Sam.

The four wolves that were once under Zara's magical control were free. They could feel the touch of their human skin and the coldness of the ground as they transformed back into their human forms. Cy and Sam rushed to their aid with coverings to conceal their naked bodies. The young ladies wept in disbelief while the young men expressed gratitude for being saved. Disoriented and feeling as though they had awoken from a dream, each youngster lifted themselves to freedom. And as for my father, he rose from the ground a bit shaky but also freed from Zara's magic. He stood by me with pride and continued to watched as I finished what I set out to accomplish.

"My magic!" cried Zara, attempting to conjure up her power yet finding nothing.

Still in denial, Zara made several attempts to draw her magic out; however, the power of the crystal was true and finite. And although Zara still had her immortality, she would live the rest of her days unable to harm another.

Lifting my hands up to the air with both crystals in my palms, I asked that my final request of the Jade Crystal come to fruition.

"No!" cried Zara as she could feel the pull of the crystal once again.

However, this time, the pull of the crystal was not toward itself. Zara was being pulled toward the gem that held no magic or value and was a simple as the blue-indigo bottle. Trapped in the fake crystal with no magic, Zara would rest for eternity. And just as it was Serena's duty to protect, so now was mine. Pulling out the Phoenix Staff once again from my bag, I waved it in a circular motion, opening up the flaming portal. Reaching inside the portal, I let go of the gem and allowed it to fall into the one place I knew would keep her hidden from all humanity. Peeking my head into the portal, I watched as the gem hit the dark water and slowly sink until it reached the sandy bottom.

"Seal," I whispered.

And just as I spoke, rocks began to interlock and form together at the side entrance where Zara's magic once swept me to the bottom. And rocks began to interlock above at the opening, sealing off all light into the old forgotten well. Nothing and no one would ever come to know what is beneath that rocky seal.

Chapter

25

O ur arrival at the mansion was not through conventional means. The youngsters who were freed from Zara's magic were given the Jeep to return to their lives, leaving us to use the Phoenix Staff to arrive at our home. One by one, we each entered the portal and walked straight into the foyer of the mansion where my mother just happened to be walking by. When she saw us all appear suddenly, her expression was not of startled fear, nor was it of concern. But it was of happiness and sheer joy. No matter how we arrived, she was relieved to have found us all home and all safe. When she saw Sam, she eagerly wrapped her arms around him. "Welcome home. I knew she would bring you back," cheered my mother.

"She did more than that, I assure you," Sam added with a smile.

"Oh, what does he mean by that?" asked my mother, turning toward my direction.

I had still not given my explanation about Sam, and I know he along with the others waited patiently enough. Standing in the foyer Cy, my father, my mother, and Sam all stared back me, eagerly awaiting what I had to say. As I looked back at all of them, I saw for the first time a glimpse of my future and smiled. I saw the Jade Crystal, the Phoenix Staff and even the book of Mystics along with the medallion of Oris all floating in each of their invisible vaults Cy created and housed in a secured room protected also by Cy's shield. I saw my mother and father raising Lilly and watching her grow into a remarkable little person full of spirit and wonder. I saw my magic develop and grow into a power that was truly meant to help and protect people. And lastly, I saw Sam never having to ever contain himself at night, never having to experience a full transformation into an animal, and never being lost to his primal anger ever again. I saw Sam finally having a home here with us in the mansion for a very, very, very long time. *Why is this? Why can this reality be true?* Sam was given the gift of an altered curse—an animal only on the inside and forever human on the outside. It was Sam's humanity that I fought for and his humanity that allowed him to be changed. This is what I was able to do. This is what Serena knew I could do. And in the midst of all this self-discovery, I also saw what was built. What Serena was a part of once now is the same for me, yet new and different. What we had now become, I suppose we were all meant to become. We were the new guardians of Avalon made up of two immortals and surrounded by family. My promise to Serena was honored, and my future or destiny was no longer sought after. It was before me and ready to be embraced.

CPSIA information can be obtained
at www.ICGtesting.com
Printed in the USA
BVHW042334021121
620519BV00001B/22